Offbeat Crimes

# ALL THE WORLD'S AN UNDEAD STAGE

ANGEL MARTINEZ

All the World's an Undead Stage
ISBN # 978-1-78686-343-0
©Copyright Angel Martinez 2018
Cover Art by Posh Gosh ©Copyright January 2018
Interior text design by Claire Siemaszkiewicz
Pride Publishing

# ALL THE WORLD'S AN UNDEAD STAGE

# Dedication

Dr. Shock, Zacherly, Wee Willie Webber and all the other hosts of B-movie horror and science fiction shows on television during my childhood — this one's your fault.

# Chapter One

"Did you finish it?" Carrington leaned out of the bathroom into the hall, ruffling his hair dry.

Erasmus poured his second cup of coffee. He was almost awake enough for guessing games. "Finish what, Mr. Cryptic?"

"The book?"

"The Cabal one? I did. Yesterday at lunch." Erasmus frowned as he checked the fridge and counted blood packets. "Is your shipment coming soon? You're almost out."

An offended sniff came from the bedroom—one of actual offense, not the kind where Carr was kidding. "You could have said. I was looking forward to discussing."

Erasmus choked on a laugh. "Would that have been before you ambushed me with octopus hands when I came through the door or while you were dragging me down onto the carpet because you wanted to be, and I quote, *filthy and do it right in the vestibule*?"

"We had all evening!"

"You fell asleep."

Carr strode out of the bedroom, uniform pressed and polished, and Erasmus couldn't help a soft, lust-filled sigh. He did love the tight fit of that uniform and it both warmed him and frustrated him to get to see Carr in it first thing most mornings. He still hadn't moved in, though that was a formality at this point. When Carr worked day shift, they stayed at his place where Erasmus could walk to work and when his vampire worked nights, Erasmus went back to his place since their schedules didn't align at all those days.

"Terribly sorry about that. I guess I was more exhausted than I realized. Inconsiderate purse snatchers running off into the sunlight."

"Weatherman says clouds all day today." Erasmus stole a soft kiss. "And at least the days are getting shorter. I did enjoy the book. Didn't know how to feel about necromancer humor but it was perfect. A very dry kind of funny. We'll have to pick up the next one. And you didn't answer the question."

"Shipment's scheduled tomorrow. In plenty of time, my dear." Carrington used the reflective front of the fridge to straighten his already straight tie. "I do wish I could take the day off with you. Maybe I should call in sick."

"You don't get sick and if you called in sunstroked, you'd be lying and feel rotten about it all day. You wouldn't be any fun at all."

"Damn you and your inevitable good sense." Carr ruined his sulk with that adorable unsure grin, the one with just a flash of fang. "Will you be here later?"

"I'm not draping myself across your sofa to watch reality TV and languishing until you return." Erasmus slipped an arm around Carr's waist and hurried on before the spark of hurt in his vampire's eyes could catch. "I'll come back when you're on your way home. Meeting my moms for lunch. Getting some errands in. I *do* have a life."

"You're a dreadful minion."

Erasmus put his hands to his cheeks in an exaggerated gasp. "I thought *you* were the minion."

Carr threw a balled-up napkin at him, scowling, though his eyes laughed. He grabbed his hat and his insulated lunch bag, swooped in for a kiss that curled Erasmus's toes, and gave a cheeky salute as he left the condo. "I'll see you tonight."

"Have a good day! Be safe!"

He said it every time Carr went off to work and every time it gave him a little shiver. *Be safe.* The wish of every spouse and partner of every police officer who had ever lived and Erasmus knew enough by now to realize it meant *I love you, come back to me whole and healthy.* Most days, nothing dangerous happened. But it only took one bad day…

Best not to think those things. It only invited trouble.

\* \* \* \*

"How's your head?" Amanda asked as she took the Sixth Street exit off the Vine Street Expressway.

"Surprisingly well this morning." Carrington couldn't help the bit of smug that crept in.

"Yeah? You looked like you were headed for a bad night after you tackled that dude. In the sun. After running three blocks. In the sun."

"I ate and slept well. Perhaps I'm becoming more acclimated these days."

Amanda's sideways glance was quick and sharp. "And you got laid."

"Certainly none of your business and I don't see how you would know. Or how that would be of any help with the sun." Carrington turned over an uncomfortable thought. "You *don't* know, do you? Manda, you can't see—"

She cut him off with a laugh. "Nah. I'd have to be at your place and really concentrating hard. It'd be way more info than I'd ever want. You're just more, you know, perky and shit the next day."

Carrington huffed. "I am not *perky*. Dreadful choice of words. Though I do wonder if sex mitigates the effects of sun exposure."

"Guess you'd have to run tests." Amanda snickered when he swatted at her. "Sorry. I'm ragging on you too hard today. Carr?"

"Yes?"

"It's good to see you happy."

Not at all the sentence he'd expected. Carrington snapped his mouth shut, unable to process a quick answer, and when nothing clever or sarcastic presented itself, he murmured, "Thank you."

She gave him an awkward pat once she'd parked in the station's lot, obviously out of words as well. Quite all right—they understood each other and Amanda wasn't the best with, as she said, *mushy stuff*.

The majority of the squad had already arrived that morning, a trend that had become more prevalent. Vance chatted in animated fashion with Shira about what he'd done with his kids that weekend. Someone had made Audacity a paper airplane to bat around, but Tim had been eyeing it. The game had become one of the kitten snatching the airplane up and racing off with it while Tim pursued in his paper ball house. Every time he caught up, she dashed off again.

Krisk lifted his huge foot to let them both race under his desk, most of his attention on his screen. Carrington didn't envy him the email cleanup after his extended hospital stay. Wolf related something to Eva and LJ that required a lot of complex gesticulation.

For a moment, Carrington allowed himself to lean in the doorway and observe, an unfamiliar sense of pride warming the space around his heart.

"Taking in the view?" Kyle stopped near him on his way in.

"Having a moment, I suppose." Carrington swallowed against a sudden lump in his throat. "Two years ago, half of them didn't like the other half. Everyone resented being here. They straggled in barely on time. Complained about everything. Now look at them."

"They grow up so fast." Kyle let out a tragic sigh, though his eyes twinkled. "I know what you mean. Believe me. I guess shared trauma goes a long way."

"Hmm. I'm certain that's a good portion of it. Where's Kash?"

"His turn for the coffee run. He'll be here in a couple." Adorable how Kyle's features lit up with such a simple mention of his husband. There were certainly more cheerful reasons than shared trauma for the increased harmony in the squad room.

Carrington made his way through the desks, careful to step around Audacity and over Tim. She'd decided the game was over and now stood on her hind legs with the paper airplane in her teeth, trying to place it atop Tim's house. Peeping encouragement, Tim leaned out and helped by patting the airplane flat with his fuzzy head and adding it to his construction.

"Hey, Carr!" Greg called from across the room. "Your mom's on line one!"

"Why does that sound like the beginning to a terrible joke?" Carrington set his lunch bag on the desk and stared at the blinking light on his office phone. "Did you tell her I'm not in yet?"

Greg shifted uncomfortably. "I'm not gonna *lie* for you. I told her you just walked in."

Carrington glanced around the squad room to determine if anyone might be a willing ally, but Jeff caught on before he could say a word. "Talk to your mother, Carr, or I'm getting on the phone and telling her you're avoiding her."

"Abandoned and friendless. I see how it is." Carrington sighed as he sank into his desk chair.

"Drama queen," Amanda muttered.

"Ice-hearted prol," he shot back, then took a deep breath before he picked up the phone. "Mom? A bit on the early side to be calling the station. All's well, I trust?"

"Carrington." She huffed and he cringed to hear himself in her mannerisms. "I wanted to catch you before you went driving about."

*Yes. That's what I do. Drive aimlessly around the city.* He hoped the eye roll didn't bleed into his voice, though Amanda snickered. "Oh, yes? How can I assist?"

As she explained in that *I have spoken, there will be no debate* voice, Carrington's optimistic energy drained from him. "I certainly hope I can depend on your help with arrangements."

"That's…" Carrington began, trying to buy himself a moment while his morning brain tried to parse this sentence. Of all the things she could have possibly said, he would never have predicted *that*. "Probably something you should clear with the lieutenant, don't you think?"

"Don't be silly. You're right there."

"I'll present your proposal but I won't make promises." Carrington cringed as he snapped a pencil in half. "Will that suffice, Mother dear?"

"It's far too early for that tone, Carrington. Let me know what Mia says."

Carrington hung up and slumped in his chair, staring at the ceiling.

"You okay?" Amanda peered around their monitors.

"Never better. I've always wanted to play go-between for my mother and Lieutenant Dunfee."

Amanda withdrew, her voice muffled as she said, "I'm not laughing. Nope."

"Hush, you," Carrington muttered.

His partner's teasing didn't bother him. His family, on the other hand, most assuredly did. They made him so tired, his controlling mother, his emotionally detached father and his idiot brother. To be fair, Mom had her moments and she *did* worry about Carrington in her own way. Her priorities just tended to be skewed.

Carrington spent roll call worrying over how to start the conversation with the lieutenant and when everyone scattered to start the day, he decided to dive in with both feet and hope there was water in the pool.

"Ma'am? Would you have a moment?"

Lieutenant Dunfee's stare could have stripped paint from a suspension bridge but her words weren't quite as harsh as he feared. "What is it you can't bring up in front of the squad, Loveless? Tell me you haven't screwed up again."

"No, ma'am. It's nothing to do with investigations." He hesitated, fighting against foot scuffing. "My mother called this morning…"

"Gods preserve us," Lieutenant Dunfee muttered. "My office."

When they'd entered the office and closed the door, he forced himself to sit straight in the chair in front of her desk rather than curl into the ball of mortification he would've preferred.

"Apologies in advance, ma'am, for any irritation or inconvenience."

"Spit it out, Loveless. The suspense is already getting on my last nerve."

"Yes, ma'am. Mother has gotten it into her head that we — the Seventy-Seventh — should have an open house of sorts. Not really an open house, since it would be by invitation, but an event where our, ah, benefactors could come for a meet and greet luncheon sort of thing."

"You mean to see how we spent their money."

Carrington shrank despite himself. "I don't think I can deny that. Apparently, Dr. Hayes had mentioned something about visiting the station the last time he and my mother had lunch. She took the thought and ran off with it. I realize it was years ago, ma'am, but we did have help…"

She waved him off with an aggravated snort. "I haven't forgotten. Damn right we owe some of the old money in this city. Irritating to have our workspace invaded but saying no would be flat out stupid. And might cost you an ear, if I know your mother."

"Probably. Possibly half my face, as well."

"I know she didn't come to you without a date." Lieutenant Dunfee turned to her screen, presumably to pull up calendars. "When does Helen want this?"

Carrington consulted the little notebook from his shirt pocket. "She mentioned the thirteenth."

Lieutenant Dunfee's eyebrows drew together. "Valbuena's due for his visit that week. Though having brass in from State is probably more good than bad."

"As if we'd specially invited the elite in just for his benefit," Carrington murmured.

"Don't get smart. Richard will be in his element. Charming the local royalty."

"Mmm." Carrington choked down all the smartass things he wanted to say about Valbuena. Not that he hated the captain with the forge of a thousand suns as he hated some of the vamps at State. No. Valbuena wasn't so bad and was a serious, competent detective. He was still dreadfully high-handed and full of himself.

"Tell her the date works and I trust her to make any arrangements she sees fit. *But—*"

"Ma'am?"

"*You* are a law enforcement officer, *not* a damn party planner, and she'd better remember it."

"I'll be abundantly clear, ma'am."

"Out. Get to work. Stop bringing me complications."

"Ma'am." Carrington touched the illusory brim of a nonexistent hat in salute and fled.

All things considered, not the worst meeting he'd ever had with Lieutenant Dunfee.

\* \* \* \*

"Hunter? It's all right. I promise." On his knees in the room LJ and Hunter shared, Carrington peered under the bed where Hunter huddled in the far corner. "No one here will hurt you."

To Carrington's relief, his mom had taken care of nearly all the arrangements for this open house luncheon and left him out of it. He would've preferred something with less fuss and fewer caterers, but it was only for a few hours. The squad room would survive. His only task now was to try to coax a spooked Hunter out from under the furniture.

"I have a theory," Jeff said from where he leaned in the doorway.

Carrington smacked his head on the bed frame trying to reach farther underneath, so his next words were sharper than necessary. "Oh, yes? I don't suppose you'd care to *share* this brilliant bit of enlightened thinking."

Jeff let out a little huff. "Not if you're going to take my head off."

"My apologies. I'm not in the best position to be civil at the moment."

"I can wait until I'm not talking to your butt."

"Fine." Carrington eased out from under the bed and sat back on his heels. "What's your thinking here?"

"When Hunter was living on her own, she was pretty careful and particular, wasn't she?"

*Living on her own* translated as *when she was homeless*, and *careful and particular* into *skilled and cautious thief* but Carrington appreciated his colleague's care with Hunter in the room. "So one is given to understand."

"I'm thinking maybe someone or several someones invited today might have been a target. Maybe Hunter's afraid of someone recognizing her and making the connection."

Carrington leaned down far enough to peer under the bed again. "Is that it, Hunter? Are you concerned that someone will recognize you from your previous life?"

Even with Hunter scrunched in the corner, she still managed a collar nod.

"Very well, then." Carrington patted the mattress. "We'll close the door, Ms. Hunter. You don't have to see anyone if you don't wish to."

A sleeve poked out from under the mattress to pat Carrington's hip. He took the hint and got to his feet to give Hunter room to wriggle out. She floated up and settled carefully on the blankets with her sleeves crossed.

"My word of honor." Carrington held up both hands. "You can lock the door behind us."

She slumped as if in relief and nodded. Then she twitched up straight, holding up a sleeve to ask them to hold on. Jeff peered over Carrington's shoulder as Hunter tugged a box out from the steamer trunk she shared with LJ. She handed the box to Carrington with a sleeve motion that appeared to mime pulling up a zipper.

"This is for LJ?" He waited for her nod. "I'll take it right out to him."

As he'd promised, he shut the door behind them to give Hunter her privacy and found LJ in the squad room with Audacity under one arm. Their kitten wore a scaled-down version of a black K-9 vest.

"Don't you look official?" Jeff let her catch one of his fingers to gnaw on.

Carrington gave her an approving nod. "It suits you. Do you like your new uniform?"

*Mew. Miii-iiw.* Audacity pedaled with all four paws until LJ set her down. She turned in an obvious modeling pose to show Carrington one side of the vest with POLICE stenciled in white block letters, then turned to display the other side with CADET FAMILIAR. If that wasn't Jason's idea, Carrington would eat his police hat *and* Amanda's.

"Outstanding, Cadet Audacity. Very sharp." Carrington kept the laughter from his voice since she was taking it all so seriously. But it was difficult in the face of such monumental cuteness. "LJ, Hunter refuses to come out but she sent you this."

He handed over the box and stayed to watch LJ ease it open by pinching the top with his sleeve. The long slender shape of the box made guessing the contents easy and Carrington wasn't disappointed when LJ held up a regulation police uniform tie. LJ stared at it for a moment — his version of staring at any rate — then gave a sharp nod before he handed the tie and box to Carrington to hold.

"You don't — " Carrington almost asked if he didn't want it but LJ's intentions became obvious when he zipped up his front and straightened his collar. "Ah. Would you like me to do the honors?"

LJ gave another nod as he held himself straight and still. Strange to see him that way. He almost never zipped himself closed and never floated completely motionless. Carrington stood behind him to get the tie on just right — easier than trying to think about tying one backward — and finished it off with the silver tie clip Hunter had provided.

"There, sir." Carrington clapped him on both shoulders. "Almost as sharp as Audacity."

LJ had no way to blush, but his front puffed out just enough to be noticeable and who would ever have predicted that? A jacket entity, former street thug and informant proud to wear police issue anything.

"Tim?" Carrington craned his neck, searching the squad room for Tim's house.

The paper sphere rolled from behind Kash's desk at speed and stopped short in front of Carrington as Tim popped out and assumed his version of attention. Not only did he have on his tiny police hat, he also wore a matching blue tie.

"Goodness. You've all taken the lieutenant's admonishment to look sharp very seriously." Carrington leaned forward for a better look. "Wherever did you get that tie? It's perfect."

Tim peeped and did a head point at Jeff, who had turned an interesting shade of pink. Sort of a dark flamingo. Not quite puce, though. *Horrid name for a color – puce.* It conjured up terrible shades of hangover rather than a hue in the reddish family.

Carrington shook the stray thoughts from his head and turned to Jeff. "How did you find such a thing?"

"I, ah, made it. There are probably ties for Ken dolls out there but I didn't think they'd fit Tim's...well, whatever fills in as Tim's neck."

"I see. Do you do tailoring?"

Jeff waved that off with a laugh. "No, no. I'm not that good. Just crafty stuff. Little things."

"He's teaching me how to knit," Vance said with a straight face as he walked past with an armload of paper for the shredder.

Carrington could only respond with an inquisitive eyebrow raise. Jeff's complexion definitely edged toward puce now.

"I knit. It's relaxing." Jeff shrugged. "Vance's anger management counselor thought it might help him."

"Reasonable. And has it?"

Jeff's soft chuckle held a tinge of chagrin. "Not at first. It's frustrating learning something new and I'm glad I used cheaper yarn 'cause a lot of it's ash now. He's getting it. I think it will."

"He has seemed more, shall we say, even-keeled lately. Though I assumed that had to do with winning joint custody."

"Carr, you just don't know." Jeff shook his head. "He was wound so damn tight for so long about losing his kids, I thought he'd shatter some days. He's getting better though and he's really trying."

*You're a far better man than I am, Jeffrey Gatling. Were he my partner, I would've killed him by now.* "Good. It's good to see him less...volatile."

Caterers and their contractors flowed in from the front hall in steady schools and swarms, though Carrington supposed one could have *either* schools *or* swarms. Otherwise, the one might drown or the other suffocate out of water. Flurries of caterers. Bustles of caterers. *Is there a collective noun for caterers?* Strange to see the squad room lined with tables covered in blue and gold cloths. Stranger still to have all of these...*strangers* present. He couldn't recall a time when there'd been more than two or three non-Seventy-Seventh people in the squad room since those first murky days when renovations had needed to be done to keep the decrepit building the city had given them from collapsing.

A more commanding presence stepped through the catering stream to interrupt Carrington's reminiscences about plumbing repairs. Parade perfect in his dress uniform, hat tucked under his arm, Captain Valbuena had arrived.

For half a breath, Carrington hung back out of habit but Lieutenant Dunfee wasn't in the room to greet him. It was his responsibility. Girding his metaphorical loins, since his physical loins and Richard Valbuena in the same sentence didn't bear thinking about, Carrington strode over to offer his hand and his concern.

"Sir. Good to see you but are you all right?"

"Quite well, Officer Loveless." Valbuena's handsome forehead crinkled in a way that didn't detract from his good looks one smidge. "Why do you ask?"

"No travel box? No rens?"

"Ah." The crinkling cleared. "Excellent cloud cover and Mina and Javier brought my travel box into the front hall. I'm afraid we thoroughly shocked some of the caterers." This last was said with a dismissive shrug that made it clear he wasn't sorry in the least.

"Good to hear—" Carrington did a delayed double take. "You actually have a ren named Mina?"

"Short for Wilhemina, which she despises. But she's heard all the jokes before, Loveless. I'd thank you not to call attention to it."

A few choice, sharp phrases lingered on the tip of Carrington's tongue. He swallowed them with difficulty. "Of course, Captain. I understand how challenging State can be sometimes."

Valbuena gave him a nod. An ambiguous acknowledgment of things they both knew. "Well, then. I *am* impressed. Everything looks inspection-ready and well in hand."

Backhanded, as compliments went, as if the captain were shocked that Carrington and his squad mates had managed such a ridiculously small feat of logistics. He hoped his tone communicated mild and unchallenging with his, "Thank you, sir." *A crowbar might help to unclench my jaw later, though.*

He was spared further uncomfortable social niceties when Wolf hurried up with a more genuine and open smile for Valbuena. "Captain! Good to see you."

"Alex!"

They clasped hands and forearms and Carrington had the impression that there would've been an impressive bone-crushing hug to go with the handshake if they hadn't been in the squad room. Their smiles were genuine—all too obvious that they actually liked each other—and the stab of dark jealousy nearly took Carrington out at the knees.

Not that he wanted either Wolf or Valbuena in a sexual or romantic sense, but he would never have that easy camaraderie with another vampire. *And isn't that the most selfish thought you've had all month? There's no other being on this green Earth like Wolf and you want to begrudge him a friend just because the cool-clique bloodsuckers were rotten to you once upon a time. Pitiful.*

He managed a wan smile and wandered off, more than happy to leave the captain in Wolf's capable hands as they chatted about arrangements. Travel box? Yes, it was back in the van now. Rens? Two, but they'd be doing some follow-up work on a case and wouldn't be lurking about the squad room. And so on.

Carrington needed to pull himself out of this strange melancholy trench he'd stumbled into and quickly. His mother was due to arrive any moment.

A snick of the office door announced Lieutenant Dunfee's emergence. In dress blues with Edgar riding on her shoulder, she was such a mix of military precision and arcane strangeness that Carrington did find a smile. As much as they butted heads, he suspected he would have fallen for her if he hadn't been entirely gay.

"You need to behave, Edgar. Hear me?" she told her familiar too softly for human ears to hear.

"Crap!" Edgar responded with a ruffle of his feathers.

"No. No cussing. No questionable language. No pranks."

"Snacks!"

"Fine. But I'll be busy. Who will you be good for if they feed you?"

"Manda!" Edgar clacked his beak. "Carr!"

She stroked his head feathers down. "You can't have Carrington. Go and ask Amanda."

Interesting. The lieutenant rarely referred to any of her officers by their first names except, apparently, with Edgar. The neon raven took flight in a flurry of bright pink and blue to land on Amanda's shoulder.

"Manda! Snacks!"

Amanda stroked his neck feathers. "Not yet, Ed. You gotta wait for guests."

"Fu—" Edgar caught himself with a disgruntled ruffle. "Stupid guests!"

"If you promise to be extra well-behaved, I'll buy you some of that dreadful jerky from the vending machine," Carrington offered as an additional bribe.

"No," Edgar croaked out. "Sucky vamp!"

Amanda tapped his beak in warning. "That's not cool, Edgar. Carr just said he'd buy you treats."

"He's not talking about me, Manda. He's staring right at Valbuena." Carrington coughed to stop a laugh from erupting. "No, Edgar. Even Captain Valbuena is off limits this afternoon. You are not to torment him, insult him or cuss at him."

"Errrr—rreh." Edgar reverted to raven speak in his frustration. Then he clacked his beak and croaked, "Promise! Snack me!"

A voice drifted in from the front of the building and Carrington stifled a sigh. Instead of taking Edgar, he took a couple of bills out of his wallet to give to Amanda. "Manda, if you would, please?"

"You don't wanna duck out for a sec? I know that look, Carr. Your mom's here, isn't she?"

"I'll be brave and hold the field. Once more unto the breach."

"Yeah. Okay. I know you're being all noble when you pull out the Shakespeare stuff." Amanda settled Edgar more comfortably on her shoulder. "C'mon, you horror-movie chicken. Let's get your snack."

*Besides, I have a cunning plan.*

Where Valbuena had parted the caterers like the Red Sea in his royal progress, Mom sent them into spinning eddies of obsequious activity. These weren't just any caterers, of course, but *her* people. Once she had a relationship with a service or contractor that satisfied her, she didn't let go and considering the entertaining she did, the caterers were right to bow and scrape. She had to be far and away their most lucrative customer.

Carrington stayed in the center of the squad room, rocking heel to toe, waiting until Mom had run through her list of verifications, queries and instructions. Naturally, once her attention was free, she zeroed in on him and juggernauted her way through the desks.

"You look tired," was her greeting. "You haven't been sleeping here again, have you?"

"Hello to you too, Mom, and no, I haven't done that in years." Not since Amanda had been assigned as his partner and he had someone he trusted to ferry him back and forth when he couldn't drive himself.

"Where's Mia? I really should say hello."

"Plenty of time for that." Carrington tucked her hand in the crook of his arm and strolled over to where Valbuena was talking to Wolf and Krisk. "Mom, I'd like to present Captain Richard Valbuena, who heads the vampire detective unit in Harrisburg. Captain, this is my mother, Helen Loveless."

Valbuena's old-world manners showed as he waited for Mom to extend her hand. Then he went so far as to bow over it. "Charmed. Though we did meet, briefly, during my previous visit to the city."

"Of course I remember, Captain. It's lovely to see you again."

Carrington murmured an, "I'll let you get reacquainted" while he sidled away. Mom was in full social plumage—all smiles and flutter with a male of the correct social class without crossing the serious flirting line. *Should keep them both out of everyone's hair for a while.*

The flurries of caterers subsided to a trickle of wait staff getting into place and shortly thereafter, the guests began to arrive—representatives of city government and the commissioner's office, certain of Mom's friends who *had* to be invited and the actual benefactors who had funded the station. A small, intimate gathering by Mom's standards but enough to transform the squad room into a maze of feet and conversation groups. All those feet.

*Tim.* The belated realization almost arrived too late. Carrington raced across the floor and scooped Tim's house up just as a spiked heel was about to back into the paper sphere. He stood there trying to smile, trying to ignore his heart slamming against his sternum, as he carefully placed Tim atop his desk.

Certainly, Tim could've rebuilt. He'd adapted so well to using paper instead of yard waste, after all. But if that heel had crunched down on the fuzzy little miscreant himself? No. That didn't bear thinking about too hard.

"Best stay elevated," Carrington murmured when Tim climbed out of his house to stare at him. How Tim managed to look surprised when he had no facial features was one of the mysteries of the universe. "You'll be much safer up here, you and your house. More at eye level, if you catch my meaning."

Tim nodded vigorously, which caused his hat to tilt. With an aggravated peep, he popped back inside his house and emerged with the hat straightened.

"Please tell me you don't have a mirror in there," Carrington whispered.

He knew quite well Tim didn't have an expedient way to answer that but the fuzzy body straightened as if he might be trying to think of one. A soft, bemused voice interrupted.

"Interesting. Is that some sort of exotic caterpillar? He reminds me of the little worm on *Sesame Street*."

Every muscle tensed to the point of pulling something as Carrington fought the urge to jump out of his skin. He'd been so focused on Tim that he hadn't heard Dr. Hayes approach. The riot of scents and sounds in the squad room helped not at all.

"Dr. Hayes." Carrington offered a hand and a warm smile. "It's good to see you. This is Tim. As far as the experts can tell us, he's neither arthropod nor annelid, though they've no educated guesses regarding how to classify him. Tim is one of our consultant entities."

"Oho. I see." Dr. Hayes adjusted his glasses to peer closer. "Something like the jackets?"

"Something of the sort." Carrington glanced over at LJ, who was managing to hold court with a group of matrons and a whiteboard. "How did you know there are multiple jackets?"

"The savage book incident at city hall," Dr. Hayes chuckled. "I wasn't there that day but several people described more than one heroic flying jacket. In whispers, naturally, so they wouldn't look like loonies."

Carrington snickered. He could easily imagine the high and mighty of society confiding such things in hushed tones, especially to Dr. Hayes, an old-money bachelor, considered an eccentric fuddy-duddy for his insistence on teaching linguistics. He was the nonthreatening, acceptable person to talk to about odd things if one were of a certain social circle.

He'd never fooled Carrington, though. Dr. Hayes was a serious scholar, not a hobbyist, and kept his chair in his department and his university connections for that reason. Eccentric, yes, but one could slice oneself on that sharp intellect if one wasn't aware.

"How are you doing these days?" Dr. Hayes turned to lean back against the desk with Carrington, bumping him with his shoulder. "We haven't seen much of you."

*We* meaning functions at the House of Loveless. "I'm…" Carrington stopped and actually thought about his answer a moment. Easy enough to say fine or doing well but polite platitudes wouldn't quite cover it any longer, would they? A little smile broke through before he could catch it. "I'm doing much better these days. Content. I might even dare to say happy."

"Excellent!" Dr. Hayes patted his shoulder instead of walloping Carrington in manly fashion as his father would have. "You had somewhat of a rough patch for a bit. I must say, I'm impressed with what you've accomplished here."

"All credit to our officers, sir." Carrington nodded to his colleagues milling about the squad room. "They're good cops and an outstanding team."

"Who would have predicted it, eh? I'd understood you were all meant to be the cast-offs."

"All too true. But odd paranormal abilities do not necessarily translate into sub-par police officers. I have two who'd nearly made or made detective prior." Carrington waved his water glass to indicate Jeff and Vikash. "And several solid, experienced patrol officers — Monroe, Zacchini, Virago, Santos — to balance out the new blood. A good mix, all in all."

"Glad to hear it, my boy. I've heard the odd rumor or two that you might have a beau, as well. A *respectable* one, I may or may not have overheard your mother say since he's a librarian. Don't suppose that helps with the contentedness?"

Carrington sipped to cover his shock. *Respectable? We've obviously reached the end times.* "It does. Very much. Enjoying the spread?"

"Ah, carefully." Dr. Hayes rubbed at his stomach. "I've had to give up salt entirely. Dreadful thing, Carrington, getting old."

Kash wandered over with Eva and after introductions, Kash walked off with Dr. Hayes as they discussed the relative merits of various constructed languages. Eva just shook her head and snagged three crab puffs from passing wait staff.

"These are really good," she said as an opening conversation gambit.

Carrington offered her a mock-offended sniff. "I'll have to take your word for it. Though Tim might like some."

Eyebrows drawn together, expression intent, Eva broke off small pieces of pastry and lined them up atop Tim's house. He let out happy little squeaks as he perused the crumb lineup and, in some meticulous and Tim-logical order, gathered the crumbs up one by one by bending his head to catch it in the fold of his neck, or at least the Tim approximations of head and neck. Little peeps and crunches emanated from Tim's paper house, the humans watching still none the wiser regarding the mystery of how exactly Tim ate.

When Tim popped back up, he'd straightened both hat and tie and he purred as he watched the gathering.

Eva popped the last of her pastry into her mouth and dusted off her hands. "That's going in the journal."

"Journal?" Carrington asked, half-distracted as his mother hooked Wolf into a conversation. *Best keep an eye on that.*

"My work journal. About what happens during shift. Weird things can be important, so I like to write them down." Eva dusted off her hands. *"Tim likes crab puffs* goes into tonight's."

"Ah." Carrington gave her a sage nod. "Things like *my new partner's sense of humor is so dry, I fainted from dehydration?"*

Eva's side-eye was so hard, Carrington wondered how he was still standing. "Kash is great. He's just quiet."

"My apologies." Carrington gave her a hint of a salute. "My own humor could use a bit of work some days. I'm glad you're getting along so well. How is aura practice coming?"

"Okay. Works best with Kyle helping. But I guess it's better?"

"Tell me what you see out there." Carrington nodded at the milling guests who had congregated around food tables, LJ and Audacity, leaving him and Eva in a lovely pocket of quiet.

Eva narrowed her eyes. She didn't quite squint, so that in itself was an improvement. "Your mom — is it okay if I read your mom?" She waited until Carrington gave her a wave to go on. "She's complicated. Red darts running everywhere. It's like a map but a 3D one with lots of different symbols on it."

Carrington sipped his water, nodding. "That's Mom. Schemes and plans at the speed of sound. Or possibly light. I suppose I've never measured."

Eva let out a choking snort, her eyes dancing. *Ah, she does laugh.*

"But very true. Who else?"

"The one in the blue suit."

"With the jeweled heels? That's Mrs. Annenberg-McLean." Carrington couldn't help a quirk of a smile at Eva's skeptical eyebrow. "I'm quite serious."

"Wow." Eva murmured. "Rich people names. She doesn't have much for aura icons. Mostly grabby hands."

Carrington had to put his water down and turn away, trying to muffle his coughs when he couldn't laugh and swallow at the same time. He waved off Eva's concern, and was calm and collected by the time he'd turned back around. "Oh, you have no idea how accurate that is."

"Not like it's a stretch." Eva scanned the guests. "Guy standing near your mom. The one in the purple shirt. Kinda looks like a cross between a professor and a stage actor."

"Lawrence Dorrance. Yes?"

"Oh my God. How does anyone take him seriously?"

"I try not to." Carrington waved his glass toward that corner of the room. "What do you see, Eva?"

"Birds. All kinds of fluttery, flying birds."

Carrington nodded. "Constantly careening from one project to another. Fitting. What about Dr. Hayes?"

Eva turned her concentration in that direction. She squinted, rubbing at her temples with both hands. "Damn it. I don't see anything."

"Stop. I'm sorry. Eva, stop." Carrington patted her shoulder. "We've pushed too hard and you've hit your limit. It was self-indulgent and I apologize."

"Not your fault. I should know when I'm getting tired, right?" Her smile was brittle around the edges but with a deep breath, she recovered. "It took up a few minutes I didn't have to be social."

Eva wandered over to talk to Amanda and Carrington took it as a subtle hint. He hadn't been terribly social himself yet. So he took a turn about the room, chatting with familiar faces, introducing himself to new ones, taking Audacity for a while so people would be inclined to ask questions about her instead of him. He even pulled out rusty social skills and intervened in a conversation between a Mr. Hardesty and Lieutenant Dunfee. Hard to say whom he was rescuing, since a storm was brewing in the lieutenant's eyes and she'd appeared about ten seconds away from braining Mr. Hardesty with the nearest stapler.

Eventually, he'd circled around to Edgar's perch, where the raven in question had been coaxed into drawing, probably by Jeff or Amanda, possibly even Krisk. He held a green marker in his beak and drew seemingly random lines on the sketchpad lying on his lectern. The constant turn of Edgar's head so he could peruse the gathering gave him away, though. Their raven was depicting the luncheon as he saw it. He set down the green marker to pick up a black one, holding it in one claw while he uncapped it with his beak.

Edgar held the marker over the center, drawing heavy, thick lines. He leaned close, cocking his head one way then the other to examine the new strokes, his concentration so complete that he dropped the marker.

His thick beak clacked in irritation, a soft *rrrrr* rising in his throat. "Sh—fu—cr—" Edgar danced from foot to foot in ever-increasing frustration. The word he finally settled on echoed in the squad room. "Feces!"

Heads turned, of course, Mom's expression exasperated, Lieutenant Dunfee's thunderous, most of the guests waffling between scandalized and amused.

Carrington sighed and picked up the marker. "It's all right, Edgar. You did your best. It wasn't a curse word, was it? Finish your drawing. It's quite good."

The rest of the afternoon was uneventful if draining. Dorrance came over to discuss Edgar, Reese Grubb buttonholed Carrington to reminisce about the old days at school and Audacity decided she'd had enough and went to sleep on Miss Stotesbury's white coat. When the guests were leaving, Carrington cringed at the nice patch of cat hair Wolf's daughter had left behind.

Lieutenant Dunfee had made her excuses half an hour earlier, citing conference calls so she could escape to her office with Captain Valbuena for the inspection part of his visit. At least the party and the hobnobbing had put the captain in a good mood. Maybe he would be less critical of case paperwork that month. The caterer flurries returned to clean up and Carrington's mother was all smiles.

"There. That went swimmingly," she said as she leaned in to kiss Carrington's cheek. "And you were so nervous about it all."

*More annoyed than nervous.* "Well done, Mom. Please thank the catering company for us."

She stayed a few minutes longer to try to bully him into coming to dinner that Sunday. When she swept out of the building, Carrington nearly collapsed with relief.

As soon as the front door clicked shut, Edgar flapped his wings, screeching, "Fuck! Shit! Piss! Cocksucking donkeybrains! Numbass! Flaming balls! Fuck!"

"Better?" Kash asked him when the barrage ended.

"Puff me!"

Kash snagged a leftover puff before the caterers could whisk the tray away and tossed it to Edgar, who caught it in his beak. He transferred the crab puff to his claw and muttered, "Rrrrr. Better."

Carrington found some solace in realizing he hadn't been the only one relieved to have their squad room back.

# Chapter Two

The *Libri Tres de Occulta Philosophia* was missing. Erasmus checked the shelf where it should have been, on either side, above, below, on the slim chance that someone had replaced it incorrectly. Library books often went astray, either through staff mis-shelving errors or a patron simply putting a book down and abandoning it in an odd spot.

Library patrons didn't browse through the Rare Books section, though. The only people who removed the books from the shelves and locked cases, were, well, librarians. People who knew better, the very people who guarded these books with jealous zeal. It didn't seem plausible that a librarian would just *misplace* one or forget to make an entry if a scholar sent through a request to see it.

The stories from Carr and his squad mates about Pecca Teecosi had intrigued him and while he hadn't been able to turn up any info on Pecca, her mother or their property yet, he thought he might look into how someone animated objects. Tempting to say animating leather jackets and cloth dogs was a unique talent of the Teecosi family, but objects taking on a life of their own had a long and varied history.

He'd started with the Teecosi family, searching for public records. The only document he uncovered was a birth registration in 1932 for a Pecca Teecosi, so it must have been a family thing. Pecca was probably named for a favorite aunt. There were no other records. No property transfers, no marriage licenses, no death certificates and no record existed of a house on that parcel of land that Erasmus could find. Really strange stuff.

So he'd decided to go after the magic end of the thread since the historical one had dead-ended — and what better place to start than Heinrich Agrippa's seminal magic work? Erasmus snickered, wondering if Carrington would've channeled his inner twelve-year-old at the word *seminal*. *Probably*. He had some odd funny-bone points and some odd ticklish spots, too. Heat joined amusement to coil in Erasmus' midsection at a random memory of Carr's pale limbs flailing as he'd tried to fend off a sneak attack. That beautiful body later stretched languid and replete on his bed…

"Off track. Getting *so* off track here." Erasmus realized he was yanking on his ear again and forced himself to stop. The important thing was that a rare seventeenth-century copy of a book wasn't where it should be. To be thorough, he began a search for the rest of the books of magic on his list.

The sixteenth-century copy of *The Munich Necromantic Handbook*, Peter de Abano's *Heptameron*, an early Latin translation of the *Picatrix*, a folio of Aleister Crowley's correspondence — Erasmus searched methodically for each of them only to find them all missing. He returned to his desk with a headache starting. None of his colleagues would be so cavalier with historic volumes as to simply *forget* to log them as in use. Rare Books librarians were even more meticulous than most specialty librarians. This had to be an odd system glitch—one he desperately hoped wasn't widespread.

He sent an inquiry out to his Rare Books colleagues anyway, just in case an unusual request had come through and someone hadn't been able to enter the information yet. It couldn't be that these items were *missing*. No one came in and out of the Rare Books department without the staff noticing. No outsider was ever left to their own devices long enough to pick case locks and stuff antiquities into a messenger bag.

*They have to be here.*

Minutes ticked by and replies trickled in, all negative. No one had received any requests for the misplaced books. No one could recall having any reason to look for them. When the last negative response hit his email, Erasmus only hesitated long enough for a wince. His colleagues would be annoyed with him—there would be a full department inventory—but they were professionals. They knew the value of those books.

He emailed the department head with a full list of the missing titles, listing the steps he'd taken so far. Half an hour later, all the Rare Books librarians received notification for a full department inventory, immediately. Erasmus shut his system down and hurried to join his colleagues by the case where Grip, the stuffed remains of Charles Dickens' pet raven, perched.

Cursing, he sent Carrington a quick text to say he wouldn't be home for dinner. The meet-and-greet of doom must have been over since Carrington answered within seconds,

*Call me when you're done. We'll go to Desi Chaat. Doesn't matter at all how late.*

It was going to be a long afternoon and evening, but at least he had a handsome, considerate vampire waiting for him at the end.

\* \* \* \*

"Will the powers that be report it as theft?" Carrington sprawled in his chair, water in hand. Even though the sun had set hours ago, he still gravitated toward shadows whenever he could, and he'd picked the table on the end of the little row outside the restaurant.

Erasmus stopped stuffing his face with *pav bhaaji* to answer, though he'd gone through three dishes and still felt like there was a hole in his midsection. "Probably tomorrow. There are procedures to follow. Inquiries to other departments. But it looks more and more like the books walked away."

"Let's hope that wasn't meant literally," Carrington muttered.

"Not ruling out anything these days."

"Why, if you don't mind my asking, were you looking for a list of books on magic?"

"Honestly?" Erasmus couldn't help a little ear tug. He hadn't done anything *wrong*, but his investigating felt a little invasive. "I was trying to find information on

Pecca. There isn't much in public records. Then I started to think about how she animated objects and was curious to see if there are records of how it's done."

"Ah." A smile twitched at one corner of Carrington's mouth. "I do love your insatiable curiosity."

Erasmus returned to devouring, while trying to think of something more to say. The drive and the first part of dinner had been perfect, since he'd just let Carrington talk about the event at the station. His less than respectful narration cheered Erasmus up considerably. Talking about his own day just made him anxious.

"Did you skip lunch again?" Carrington had on his frown of disapproval. Too bad it was an adorable frown that Erasmus had trouble taking seriously.

"Mm-hmm," Erasmus managed while chewing. "Was busy."

Carrington *tsked*, a real one, not a teasing one. "That can't be good for you. You need fuel."

"Says the vamp who doesn't eat when he's tired or depressed."

"Ras, that's diff—"

"No." Erasmus put his fork down. "No, it's not. I'm sorry you get unhappy about drinking blood sometimes, but it's just food."

"Then I shouldn't have to remind you to eat lunch, either."

"So we're both hypocrites." Erasmus hid a smile in polishing off his food. "At least when we're worried."

"Would you like something else?" Carrington gestured with his glass toward the order window.

"Part of me does, but better not. I won't get any sleep tonight if I stuff myself more."

Carrington rose and stretched, a tempting strip of pale skin peeking out between jeans and Henley. "Would you care for a walk, then? Perhaps settle your system a bit."

"A constitutional, Mr. Loveless? How old-fashioned of you."

Erasmus got the laugh he'd been after—a surprised one that warmed his heart. Carr laughed more than he used to, but it was still rare for that warm, sputtering, uninhibited chuckle to get away from him.

They strolled south a couple of blocks, walking close but with hands tucked in jacket pockets. Shame had nothing to do with it, merely caution at night in the city. Carrington always said he didn't care about his own safety—vampire strength trumped even a small gang of humans—but he didn't want Erasmus hurt because of him. Sweet, though Erasmus also knew he wasn't the macho sort who hunted for trouble and the department wasn't happy with cops who got into fights.

On Woodland Avenue, they turned east to walk along the cemetery. Creepy maybe, but Woodland was both historic and beautiful, boasting well-kept gardens and events. In the daytime. Carrington walked with his head up, eyes half-closed as he scented the gardens.

"You know it's a little cliché for vampires to like cemeteries, don't you?"

"Sometimes clichés are true." Carrington bumped shoulders with him. "My mother used to be on the historic preservation board. Spent a good deal of time in that cemetery as a child during garden parties. Wandering—"

His head jerked around toward the stone wall, nostrils flared.

"Carr?" Erasmus whispered. "What is it?"

"Freshly dug earth..."

"It is a cemetery. They still sell plots here, don't they?"

Carrington shook his head hard as if trying to clear it. "They do. But there's something...*gah*, foul about it. A fresh burial site wouldn't smell like that."

In a blur of motion, Carrington vaulted the wall, leaving Erasmus gaping on the sidewalk. He strained for every sound, though Carrington could be completely silent while stalking. He was just checking up and down the street for witnesses, debating trying to scramble over the wall, when a muffled curse reached him.

Erasmus stilled, heart leaping. "Carr?"

"I'm fine. Stay there!"

A bit of rustling, then Carrington leaped back over to join Erasmus in the light of the streetlamps. He was pulling out his phone, an angry frown creasing his forehead.

"What is it? What happened?"

"Some cretin dug up a couple of graves. Just be a second, my dear. I need to call this in."

Fighting shivers, Erasmus stuffed his hands harder into his pockets as he listened to Carrington report the vandalism in clipped, succinct sentences. In full protective mode, he even discarded his caution about touching out on the street and threw an arm around Erasmus as they waited for the patrol car.

"You're shaking."

"Sorry. I'm okay." Erasmus leaned in to try to stop the shivers. "My brain went there, I guess."

"Forgive me." Carrington pulled him in to kiss the top of his head. "I shouldn't have been so impulsive and abrupt."

"Was it bad? The bodies?"

"Hmm." Carrington's frown returned, though it suggested more puzzlement than anger. "The graves were disturbed and there appeared to be coffin remains. But no bodies. Odd. It's not as if we have resurrection men any longer. I did find this."

He pulled an object in a plastic bag out of his pocket and Erasmus had to stifle a snicker. "You carry evidence bags off duty?"

Even in the low light, Erasmus could pick out the high spots of color on Carrington's cheeks. "Well. Yes. Just in case."

"Boy Scout."

Carrington didn't even bother with a comeback, indicating a level of rattled that didn't make Erasmus any happier. He glanced at the contents of the bag — a cufflink. An expensive-looking cufflink, with a silver or platinum skull and what could have been diamonds for eyes.

"That's certainly interesting. Do you think it came from one of the graves?"

"I'm not certain. Probably not, since it's relatively clean. But I can't help the feeling I've seen it before." As the squad car pulled up, Carrington untangled himself and walked over to give his report.

The desecration of strangers' graves was distressing, but really nothing to do with him. Erasmus stood in the cycling blue and red lights of the squad car flashing blood and water on the pavement and wondered why he couldn't stop shaking.

\* \* \* \*

"You're really stuck on this, huh?" Amanda leaned around Carrington's computer screen late the next afternoon. "Like that thing where you get hold of something and can't let go."

"Obsessed?"

"That."

Carrington squinted at the images on the screen. Some were close to the cufflink's design, but not quite. "I'm not obsessed. I just know I've seen it before and I wish I could recall."

A pat on his pants leg pulled his attention from the computer. Audacity stood on her hind legs, patting at him to lift her up with an impatient *miiw*. Carrington obliged so she wouldn't start climbing him — leaving interesting pulls and holes in his uniform pants — and set her on the desk beside his keyboard.

"Oof. You're getting big." True in a relative sense, though she was still kitten-proportioned. "What can I do for you, Cadet Audacity?"

Audacity tilted her head at the screen and batted at one of the images of skull cufflinks.

"Hmm. Not precisely like that one. Similar."

*Mehh-reh?* Audacity turned to peer up at him expectantly.

Carrington opened his hands, palms up. "I'm afraid I don't have it to show you. Another district has it in their evidence room."

After another head tilt, she yanked Carrington's notebook from underneath the desk phone, leaped off the desk with an ungraceful kitten scramble and thud, and raced over to Jeff's desk where she patted at Jeff's leg.

"What's up, little girl?" Jeff peered over the edge of his desk. "Whose —"

He cut off when Audacity dropped the notepad at Jeff's feet and dashed away again. She raced to her dad's desk, climbed the little set of box stairs Wolf had made for her and stole a pen from beside his keyboard.

"Make sure you bring that back, sweetie," Wolf called after her.

*Rewr*, was all Audacity managed with her teeth full of pen. She dropped it on top of the notepad and gazed up at Jeff with her arresting blue eyes.

Jeff rubbed at the side of his face and took a guess. "You want me to write something?"

*Rrrrrrrrr.*

"Okay, no. You want me to draw something?"

Audacity sat up on her haunches batting the air with both forepaws. *Miiii-reh.* With his usual good-humored patience, Jeff followed Audacity back over and Carrington found himself describing the object for Jeff to draw.

"Police sketch of a cufflink. That's gotta be a first," Amanda muttered from her side of the desk.

But Audacity was pleased and took the drawing to her 'desk' – her box under her dad's desk – presumably to study it further.

"Central dispatch has a PPI at Blue Bell Park," Kyle called out from his desk.

Carrington made a quick mental inventory of who was working on what. "Jeff, Vance, take that one, please. Probably just another fox, but let's be thorough. Oh, and if it is a fox, tell the nice civilians that sometimes a red fox is just a red fox and to stop watching so much anime."

"What's he talking about?" Vance murmured to his partner.

Jeff chuckled. "I'll explain on the way. Nice day for a walk in the park, at least."

Audacity stayed under her desk until booted footsteps rang down the front hallway. Upon hearing them, she poked her head out of her little office, ears perked forward, then zipped across the squad room.

*Mewmewmewmewmewmewmew!*

By the enthusiastic greeting, there couldn't be any doubts regarding the identity of their visitor. Sure enough, Jason strode in, laughing as Audacity ran up to him, patted his leg with her paw then galloped back to her dad's desk, still talking nonstop.

"Yes, I see your Uncle Jason, sweetie." Alex scooped her up to place her on top of the desk, as he stood to accept a kiss from Jason. "Hey. Did I forget something?"

"No, but a certain cadet did." Jason pulled a rolled-up object out of his inside jacket pocket. "The department gave you a uniform, Audi. You really should wear it to work."

She sat prim and proper, tail curled around her paws. *Mreh.*

"All right, we'll try to remember, too." Jason scritched below her chin, which she leaned into with abandon. "Gotta run. Have some other kittens to see to today."

Audacity let out a short kitten growl.

"I'm sure Jason won't love them as much as he loves you. Don't be selfish, sweetie," Alex said with a frown. "Other kittens need help sometimes, too."

"And you're the kitten I come home to." Jason's expression was far too serious. "I'll see you both at dinner."

With kisses for both of his police personnel, Jason waved to the squad and hurried out again. Adorable, the three of them, even more so since Alex would practically glow for the rest of the day. He helped Audacity into her vest, then went back to his paperwork when she returned to hers under the desk.

Carrington was about to say something about kitten hunches when the lieutenant's voice crackled through the radios and the squad room intercom simultaneously.

*"All available units, proceed to Orange Trail in Blue Bell Park by Walnut Lane Bridge. Officer down. Repeat, officer down. Orange Trail by Walnut Lane Bridge."*

Out of his chair before the first 'officer down' had finished, Carrington raced for the door. Amanda would be close behind but he could have the car started by the time she caught up. While the officer hadn't been specified, and wouldn't be over radio communications, there weren't too many possibilities with only Vance and Jeff still out of the squad room.

"Jesus, what's Virago done now?" Amanda huffed as she flung herself into the passenger seat.

Carrington took it as a rhetorical question and concentrated on getting out of the lot without endangering the rest of their squad as they raced to their respective cars. Wolf and Krisk peeled out right behind them as Carrington switched on the lights and siren.

Amanda got on the radio. "Unit One responding, Code Three."

The response with lights and sirens code repeated from the four cars behind them as Carrington raced off north and west, toward Fairmount and then Blue Bell Park beyond where the old concrete arch of the Walnut Lane Bridge spanned the Wissahickon. Both a beautiful and ill-omened spot—the bridge itself was a lovely piece of engineering but it had been host to numerous deaths over the years.

Not that Carrington believed places truly absorbed tragedy. Not too much, at any rate.

By the time they pulled into the Blue Bell Park lot, he'd mapped out a quick route with Amanda. This bridge was too high to park at the top and scramble down an embankment. Carrington might have survived the fall, but none of the others would. They left the car and headed out through the trees toward Orange Trail. A jog of no more than four hundred feet, but it felt longer crashing through shrubs and underbrush.

"Couldn't have picked a better spot, could they?" Amanda grumbled behind Carrington. "Better not be any freaking poison ivy."

"Hush, Manda. Trying to listen."

Listen *and* smell if he was going for full disclosure. He had Jeff and Vance's scents already, and he concentrated hard on what sounds he could pick up over their passage through the woods — any sound of struggle or distress.

The relative quiet almost made him more anxious than the echoes of a firefight would have. Several disturbing scents undercut Jeff's and Vance's — smoke, rot and something acrid he couldn't identify. Carrington leaped a fallen log and hit the dirt path of Orange Trail at a sprint, hand on his weapon. Amanda cursed a blue streak behind him but he knew he wouldn't hit the scene alone. An unmistakable growl was gaining on him as Alex traded stealth for speed and came crashing through the brush.

Glimpses of gray stonework flashed between the leaves as Carrington barreled up the path. They were still ahead of him. His nose didn't lie but he didn't have them in sight until he was nearly under the looming arch of the bridge. Finding them didn't make him any happier.

Jeff lay sprawled on his back just off the path. Pale and shaking, Vance knelt beside him with a hand on his shoulder. A little farther on lay another figure – a terribly still and distorted figure that appeared to be missing part of its head.

*No pre-judgments. No conclusion jumping. But, oh, Vance, what in gods' names have you done?*

"Vance, what are we looking at here?" Carrington asked as he slowed his steps for a more cautious approach. When Vance only stared at the ground, glassy-eyed, Carrington barked out, "Virago! What's the situation?"

"Carr…" Vance twitched and glanced up. "Jeff…it attacked Jeff. Pulled him down. Tried to…something. I don't fucking know. Maybe eat him. I thought…fire. But it kept coming. Fireball…at its head."

"You keep saying *it*. The body looks human to me. Male from here."

Vance shrugged and shivered. "Might've been. Once."

"Jeff?"

Their downed officer lifted a finger and croaked out, "Present and accounted for. Hit my head on the way down."

"Jeff, stay down. Vance, sit tight." Carrington gave his shoulder a pat and strode to where Wolf leaned over the body. "Alex? Observations?"

Wolf spun away from the body with a disgusted sound before sneezing violently. "*Ugh.* That's awful."

At close range, Carrington knew exactly what Wolf meant. He swallowed against nausea as an overpowering scent of rot hit him. "That can't possibly have attacked Jeff. Whatever it was, it's been dead quite some time."

"Hell, yeah," Wolf growled. "But the shoes, Carr."

Holding his sleeve to his nose, Carrington crouched for a more thorough inspection. The body had charring along the right side, probably from Vance's initial strike, and half its head had been all but obliterated in the fireball. Both clothes and flesh were in an advanced state of decay, tatters that were indistinguishably cloth or muscle tissue hanging off bones. The shoes, though, had obviously been good leather at one time and exhibited a better state of preservation, the once-expensive soles covered in river mud when nothing else on the body was.

"It appears to have been walking," Carrington murmured.

Wolf sneezed again. "Yeah. But that can't be, right?"

Soft voices drifted to them from where Vikash had caught up and was talking to Vance. Vikash repeated the concerned shoulder pat and wandered over to Carrington. "That…is a corpse. Vance believes he killed a corpse?"

"Apparently." Carrington shifted uncomfortably, arms crossed over his chest. "I'm not discounting it yet."

"We calling crime scene folks?" Amanda peered over his shoulder at the scene.

When Carrington glanced over to Vikash, he held both hands up and took a step back. "Not my call."

"Kash." Carrington suppressed a sigh. "I *am* permitted to consult and I *do* value your opinion—"

Kyle meandered over, shaking his head. "Okay. I'm confused. Vance fireballed a moldy corpse?"

"Yes." He was not repeating the whole story every time someone caught up to them at the crime scene. "We've been along that route several times now. Let me think."

"Dr. Moreau," Vikash muttered.

Carrington nodded slowly. "Yes. A far better choice. Manda, could you—"

"Already calling." Amanda gestured with her phone. "Guess she better bring a body bag."

Disturbed graves, possible walking corpses—the implications were beyond disturbing. Carrington returned to crouch beside Jeff while they waited for Dr. Moreau. "Take me through it if you can. From the beginning."

"We had a call..." Jeff held a hand out to Vance. "Help me up. I feel ridiculous."

"Carr said—"

"Carr's right there and can probably speak for himself. I'm all right." Once Jeff was more or less sitting upright, he went on. "A call about a bridge troll. I don't know what I was expecting but by now I wasn't ruling out an actual bridge troll. Vance and I came down the trails from the parking lot and we encountered two people who said they'd seen something strange lurking under the bridge. We'd just turned that last corner when the zombie—"

"Zombie," Carrington repeated, not at all happy that someone had finally said it.

"I don't know what else to call it. It looked like it crawled out of a decades-old grave." Jeff drew a careful breath. "Anyway, it leaped out of the bushes behind me, screaming things, and grabbed me by the shoulders. I lost my balance and went down. Vance fought it off."

"Do you recall what it was screaming? Was it intelligible?"

Jeff rubbed the side of his head gingerly. "I caught some words but they didn't make much sense. Something about Mr. Bunbury making up his mind about living or dying."

"Something about shilly-shallying," Vance muttered. "Whatever the fuck *that* means."

Something about the combination of words sounded terribly familiar, though Carrington couldn't quite coax the *what* to the surface. "Is Bunbury a name either of you know?"

Jeff leaned back on one arm, his complexion decidedly greenish. "No. Honestly, it sounds like something from a Monty Python sketch."

Another horrible thought sprang up and slapped Carrington across the face. He shrugged out of his jacket to fold it and put it behind Jeff. "Probably best not to be sitting up just yet. The, ah, zombie didn't bite you, did it?"

"That makes me feel tons better, Carr." Jeff lay back down with a groan. "Shades of *28 Days Later*. No, it didn't. It grabbed me, and I never want to feel bony zombie fingers on me again, but it didn't get a chance to bite me before Vance went all *flame on*."

Vance didn't even bristle at the comment, still blinking in a distracted, thousand-yard-stare sort of way. Slowly, Carrington reached out to shake his knee. "Vance."

He reacted with a twitch and a choked-off cry. His hands shook as he held them in front of him. "I killed him. Took off half his head with a fucking fireball. Killed someone just like they always said I would."

"Hey, hey, Virago, look at me," Amanda demanded from his other side. "You were okay taking care of that dust bunny."

Vance pulled in a shuddering breath. "That was a monster."

"Yeah. And you saved people." Amanda waved a hand at Jeff. "Now you saved your partner. That thing wasn't a person any more than I'm a bowl of rice pudding. Not anymore."

"You mean you used to be a bowl of rice pudding?" Jeff managed with a straight face.

"Smartass. Vance knows what I mean."

Vance only nodded, and went back to staring at his hands. With misgivings piling on anxieties, Carrington rose and murmured in Amanda's ear, "Are you getting anything from the site?"

"Not much. I'm seeing the whatever thing come at them out of the bushes. Grabs Jeff by the shoulders and looks like it's trying to drag him away."

*Well, it couldn't be easy, could it?* "Nothing else?"

"Couple squirrels were here just before that." Amanda shrugged.

"You're not suggesting squirrels were involved, are you?"

"The way things've been going this year? Hell, I'm not gonna say we *don't* have evil genius squirrels in this city."

Carrington shuddered. "Heaven forfend."

Within fifteen minutes, Dr. Moreau arrived with Greg and Shira helping her carry equipment from the car. She performed a cursory examination of the body, then had several officers help her bag the remains.

Conclusions would have to wait until she had access to her lab. One look at Jeff and Vance, and she ordered them both to the ER.

"Officer Loveless." She stopped by Carrington, her ever-restless hands twisting the handle of her valise. "Did any civilians report being in close proximity to the entity?"

"Not that we've heard, ma'am. Sightings only from the witnesses Officers Virago and Gatling interviewed."

"Good. Good." She gazed out over the river, still speaking softly. "I know nothing at this point, you understand. But I want those two under close observation until I do know more."

"Doctor, you can't believe in zombie viruses. That's nothing but an old movie trope."

"Yes. So far. But if you live long enough, all things are possible."

She followed the body bag Wolf and Krisk were hauling back to her van and left Carrington standing on the leaf-dappled path, wishing cryptic comments would be outlawed for the duration.

# Chapter Three

"So it was a zombie?" Erasmus asked as he ladled beef stew into a bowl for himself, then grabbed a blood bag for Carrington, who had collapsed in a freshly-showered vampire heap on the sofa.

"Dr. Moreau says she would rather not give it such a fraught and imprecise name." Carrington stretched his feet out under the coffee table as he hugged a cushion to his chest. Erasmus hadn't seen him so upset since the night they'd had their not-quite-breakup. "She does confirm that it was an animated corpse, male, probably middle-aged, buried about forty years ago. It had to have been in a coffin, she insists, to retain some preservation of clothing and other tissues."

"That's... That's horrific." Erasmus put their dinner on the table, tugging at his ear while he thought. "But that means someone had to open the coffin, right?"

"One assumes." Carrington reached for his blood but didn't seem eager to drink it. "I'm not sure which scenario is worse — animated corpses with or without the interference of human agency."

Erasmus ate slowly, trying to separate his food from the words *animated corpse*. "Did she know what caused it? Strange bacteria? Interstellar interference?"

"I suppose I should be pleased that we're not looking at a zombie pandemic. Neither of those. There were, however, definite lingering traces of magic. Wolf could still smell it and I felt a hint of something as well."

"Holy crap." Erasmus's spoon clattered against his bowl as he came to a horrified realization. "Necromancy."

"Yes, that generally involves —" Carrington surged up to take his hand. "Ras, what is it? What did you think of?"

"I — I didn't make the connection before. Because the zombies are a little shocking." Ras placed the bowl on the table with shaking fingers. "The missing books. From my department. The whole list of materials from history's most powerful mages. Some of them — Well, some were huge tomes of magic. Anything could be in those. But others were *about* necromancy."

"Were they?" Carrington's hand tightened a fraction. "*Was* the theft reported yet?"

Erasmus shook his head. "Books can be mis-shelved, borrowed without proper documentation, moved without all channels updated. We have to be sure they're not in the building somewhere before we can report it. But we went through the checks today without finding them."

"You believe they were stolen, don't you?"

"I don't know what to believe." Erasmus poked at the blood bag. "You need your dinner. You're exhausted.

But, yes, I don't think it's a coincidence. *That* part of the collection going missing."

"Hmm." Carrington sank back against the cushions, stuck his straw in the convenient port and began to drink. "Can't imagine a normal thief walking out with anything from your department. I'd like some of our officers to come by tomorrow to see if they detect anything unusual." *Sip. Sip. Sip.* "Now if I could only dredge up what the corpse was yelling."

"If we'd just met, those words might've made me run far and fast." Erasmus chuckled, though it was only funny in a horrible, dark way. "I didn't realize it spoke."

"Then I'm luckier than I deserve that we're not meeting now. It said something about Mr. Bunbury making up his mind about dying, according to Jeff."

Erasmus pulled out his phone. "That's what the internet's for, Carr. So you don't have to keep beating up your poor tired brain."

"Don't discount the strange recesses of my brain."

"Never." Erasmus squeezed Carrington's thigh. "Appears to be from *The Importance of Being Earnest.*"

"Ah. That's why it sounded familiar." Carrington sipped some more and twined the fingers of his free hand with Erasmus'. "Why in the world was a corpse shouting lines from an Oscar Wilde play?"

"I'd suggest that it's some last bits of whatever he was storing in his neurons, but I bet his brain rotted away a long time ago."

A last slurp heralded Carrington finishing his dinner. "Now it's your turn. Don't waste away on me." He waited until Erasmus, without much enthusiasm, had picked up his bowl again. "And if you say anything about old actors never dying, I'm going to bed and locking you out."

"Sure. That would last about five minutes until guilt starts eating you alive."

Carrington sniffed — the short, acerbic one that wasn't serious. "I'm glad to know you think so little of my fortitude." He contradicted any pretended offense by stretching out on the sofa with his head on Erasmus' thigh. "I have far too much to do tomorrow to lie awake in guilt-ridden anxiety."

After a few difficult bites of stew that suddenly tasted like sand and cardboard, Erasmus asked, "You'll be careful? I mean, this all sounds like a new level of dangerous."

"I do my best. Truly. Necromancers are uncharted territory for me, though." Carrington sighed and nuzzled at the crook of Erasmus' thigh, purring. In a dramatic *sotto voce*, he said, "Take me away from all this *death*."

"Really, hon? A Dracula movie quote?"

"It's a very passionate scene." The nuzzling ventured further inward.

"Until the handsome vampire collapses in a pile of rats, sure."

"I promise not to devolve into a pile, basket or bushel of any sort of rodents. Even if vampires had the ability, mine would probably skew toward hamsters or chinchillas." Carrington punctuated the last word by burying his face in Erasmus' crotch.

"Hey!" Erasmus couldn't help his hips bucking as he laughed. "You wanted me to finish dinner. Sending mixed messages here."

"Terribly sorry. You smell so good." Carrington's voice vibrated against Erasmus' now-very-interested and uncomfortably trapped cock, which made squirming just about mandatory.

Erasmus seized enough of Carrington's hair to make him lie still. "How about you go get ready while I eat? Maybe see if you brought your cuffs home."

Under his fingers, Carrington went from unmoving to tense and Erasmus worried that he'd said the wrong thing.

"I have them." The hoarse whisper still could've been Carrington excited or upset. "I'm not entirely... It's not as if..."

"Carr." Erasmus curled over to kiss his shoulder. "It's just cuffs and only if you want them. If it's no, you need to say. We're not negotiating anything more than that."

Carrington rolled onto his back, his eyes sending out *guarded* and *hopeful* in an endearing mix. "Fair enough. I'll meet you in the bedroom. Don't cheat and put the stew back."

*He knows me too well.* Erasmus snickered and kept eating as he watched Carrington saunter down the hall, pulling his T-shirt off for a tantalizing glimpse of pale skin over hard muscle before he wandered into the bathroom. Maybe this would turn out to be that one step too far for Carrington. He enjoyed the feeling of being held down, even if they both knew it was a polite fiction. He liked someone else taking control in the bedroom, relaxing as he never did otherwise. It made Erasmus' heart melt—the unquestioning trust Carrington gave him, the way he let go when he didn't need to make decisions about that one part of his complicated life.

Maybe something softer—like a bathrobe tie—would've been better to start with, but Erasmus had a hunch and his Carr-hunches were usually good ones.

He took his time, finished every scrap of dinner, put the rest in the fridge and washed his dishes. Not that Carrington needed a lot of prep time. His diet made that part easier. Still, anticipation helped things along.

By the time he reached the bedroom, Carrington was stark naked and kneeling on the covers. Whether the submissive posture was conscious or not, he was heartbreakingly beautiful, moon-white against the velvet black of Carrington's comforter. He knew his vampire needed him to take charge, so he fought hard against a sudden wave of overwhelmed shyness and forced himself *not* to tug on his damn ear.

"Hey, there." *Oh, smooth, Graham. Good job.*

The only movement in response was one dark eyebrow leaping up Carrington's forehead. Erasmus wondered if he knew that his mother sometimes wore that same expression. *Not* that this was a good time to be thinking of his lover's mom.

Carrington cleared his throat. "Are you staying dressed?"

"Do you want me to?"

"I'd prefer not." The deep, husky growl was back in Carrington's voice.

Some of the strange awkwardness fell away under the simmer of Carrington's gaze and Erasmus broke into a grin as he struggled out of his dress shirt without undoing the buttons. "Good. I'm tired of pants today."

That got half a smile, though Carrington still practically vibrated with tension. The cuffs lay beside him, one neatly stacked on the other, keys beside them, and again, whether he realized it or not, he was leaning away from them.

Erasmus yanked off the rest of his clothes before he hurried to the bed and took Carrington's face between his hands. "Carr, sweetheart, I need a hard *yes* or *no* here. You won't hurt my feelings. Do you want the cuffs?"

"I think—" Carrington swallowed audibly but the heat in his eyes ramped up as he said, "Yes."

"Thank you."

Erasmus didn't say more, but he thought it was clear—*thank you for trusting me*. He climbed onto the bed behind Carrington, one hand in constant contact, the other gathering up the cuffs. Shivers whispered along Carrington's muscles as Erasmus stroked his back in broad, soothing circles.

"Ras?"

The word wavered so Erasmus wrapped his arms around Carrington's ribcage from behind. "Yes?"

"This is lovely, but are you going to *progress* to anything?"

"It's fun to make you wait." Erasmus laughed at the low, disgruntled growl before kissing his way across Carrington's broad shoulders. "But not forever. You know that." He eased an arm out to grab the cuffs, moving his kisses to Carrington's right arm as he clicked the cuff in place. "Anytime this isn't right, you tell me, okay?"

"I thought it might be amusing to have a complete and utter meltdown instead."

*Good.* Gentle bits of snark meant Carrington was on board with this and not freaking out. "You do and I'm canceling our night at the opera."

"That would be a tragedy. I suppose I'll simply need to behave sensibly."

Erasmus chuckled, then stopped himself before he clicked the second cuff shut. "Speaking of sensible, let's get you positioned before you can't use your hands anymore."

"I'm at your disposal." Carrington gave him a quirk of a smile. "Do with me as you will."

"You make it sound so drastic. Here."

Erasmus urged him to lie on his front, then had a better idea and pulled him by the hips until he lay bent face down over the end of the bed. The bed was a few inches too high so both kneeling and feet-on-the-floor were awkward, but the ornamental bolster from the head of the bed solved that so Carrington could kneel comfortably.

When Carrington stopped squirming, Erasmus set his hand on the small of Carrington's back and fastened the second cuff in place. Carrington moaned and ground his cock against the comforter but the tense set of his shoulders relaxed, the furrows smoothing from his forehead.

*Even better.* He leaned in to kiss a line down Carrington's back, breathing in the freshly showered vampire scent of soap and what he'd come to think of as waterfall — cool and mineral, bracing. Strange things one learned sleeping with a vamp. They didn't sweat and only had a noticeable, sharp citrus scent when they were injured or starving.

Guilt ate at Erasmus sometimes that he found the scent pleasant, but maybe better that he wasn't repulsed when Carrington was in distress. Nor had he mentioned that he could detect it. It helped him figure out when Carrington was fibbing about being fine.

A kiss to the dimple above Carrington's ass cheeks had him panting and Erasmus decided not to tease him too much. He was obviously enjoying this — maybe too much for a long foreplay session. With one hand on

Carrington's shoulder, he eased around the end of the bed to snag the lube from the nightstand drawer.

He dropped the lube beside Carrington's hip so he could stroke down his hard-muscled back with both hands, stopping to knead and caress that gorgeous butt. "Do you know how amazing you look right now?"

"Trussed up as if I'm ready for a holding cell?"

Erasmus laughed. "No. You're so...focused, but so pliable. It does all kinds of things to me, you just...letting go."

"Ras, I —" Carrington cut himself off with an audible swallow. "Please don't make me wait."

"I guess since you're being so polite." Erasmus squeezed lube out at the top of Carrington's ass crack and stifled a snicker at his hiss. "Cold even for you?"

"Just slightly. I'm not too cold for you, am I? Since it's no longer summer?"

"Of course not. It's not like your condo doesn't have heat, you know."

Erasmus slid a finger inside, his cock jumping at Carrington's moan and twitch. He lubed his impatient erection with his free hand while he bent over to use his lips for sucking kisses along Carrington's shoulders instead of words.

Sliding inside that cool sheath was like coming home — so familiar, so wonderful, and still it tugged sharply at something at his core, almost to the point of tears, for what the universe allowed him to have — this man, who risked his life to keep others safe, this vampire, who could have picked from a cotillion of eager candidates.

*And what he chooses, every day, is a skinny librarian.*

Carrington's eager groan brought him back into sharper focus. "Do you...should I stay still?"

Erasmus sank just a hair deeper before he began to thrust. "No, hon. God, no. Move. Squirm. Whatever you need."

The cuffs dug into Erasmus' skin where he lay on them, but he didn't care. It added a little bite to everything as Carrington moved as requested, powerful muscles heaving and bucking under him. They synced thrusts after a few wild misses and found a rhythm of ferocious abandon that had Erasmus gasping.

Kneeling wasn't the best position for Erasmus' bad leg — the one the dust monster had chewed on — but he barely felt the ache amid the delicious hurricane that was Carrington losing himself to passion. He slid an arm under Carrington, desperate for more skin to skin contact, to feel the slow beat of Carrington's heart against his.

"Please say you're close," Carrington whispered, his eyes squeezed shut.

"Close... So close," Erasmus panted out. "Don't wait for me."

With a forceful buck that lifted Erasmus from the bed, Carrington came with sharp, escalating cries and exquisite contractions around Erasmus' cock. *Nope. Nobody has to wait.* Erasmus' vision darkened around the edges as he came hard, his brain whiting out from the overload of pleasure.

He waited until Carrington had stopped his desperate squirming before he eased out, then collapsed on his side. Instant sleep tempted him, but that would've been worse than rude. Somehow, he found the energy to unlock the cuffs then help his vampire up onto the bed and under the covers.

"Sorry. I think we made a mess of your comforter," he murmured as Carrington nestled into his arms.

"It's certainly washable," came the sleepy response. "Ras?"

"I'm right here."

"You make me feel so utterly, completely safe. Maybe that's not terribly romantic. But it's entirely true."

"From you? It is romantic." Erasmus turned his head to kiss the soft hair tickling his cheek. "Thank you."

* * * *

*Why couldn't I say it?* Carrington stared at his computer screen the next morning as he waited for roll call. He had plenty of other things to occupy his attention, of course, but he kept coming back to the night before.

He'd nearly said it, in a haze of overexcited passion. *Ras, I...* Then he'd cut off the words and swallowed them like tiny shards of glass. *I love you.* While it was true—oh yes, he did love Erasmus Graham with every cell in his body—he couldn't say it yet.

"You're a coward, Loveless, pure and simple," he muttered to his keyboard. Because he waited for confirmation, waited to be sure, waited for it all to end in some horrible way that would be his fault—he couldn't say it.

"Carr, you coming?"

He glanced up in confusion to find Amanda hovering over him. She pointed to the clock.

"Oh. Yes. Gathering tufts of wool, I'm afraid."

"I'm gonna guess that means you zoned out." Amanda gave him a heavy clout to the shoulder. "Get your brain moving, Loveless. Your show this morning."

He nodded absently and gathered up his file. Everyone had assembled by the time he reached roll call, including Jeff, who probably should have taken the day off. The click of the lieutenant's heels wasn't far behind him. It was his show, as Amanda had said. Lieutenant Dunfee had pulled him into her office first thing that morning to hash through things, and she had said it was time he started acting more like a duty sergeant and less like a lump in one of the folding chairs during roll call.

*Fair enough.* The weird was once again afoot and he could delump himself for that.

Lieutenant Dunfee began the morning with the not unwarranted question, "Gatling, why are you here?"

Jeff's sigh was probably audible only to Carrington and Alex. "Dr. Moreau cleared me for light duty, ma'am. I'd rather be here than alone in my apartment, if that's all right."

"One of the better excuses I've heard. What's your excuse, Virago? Weren't you supposed to take a day?"

"Ma'am, I— I'd just be inside my own head all day." Vance's chin came up in a small show of defiance. "Dr. Moreau said it was up to me."

"Do *not* push yourself unduly. If things aren't feeling right, you say so." The lieutenant huffed and moved aside. "Loveless, podium's yours."

Since Jeff was here, Carrington had swiftly reshuffled things and was still writing notes to himself by the time he reached the lectern. "Good morning. We have several disparate items that have made their way, tangentially or directly, to this department—"

"Aw, man. Does this have to sound like a dictionary, Carr?" Vance muttered.

"I could try to speak in words of one syllable—no, I've already failed." Carrington put his notes down and gripped the lectern with both hands. "I'll be direct, though. These incidents don't appear important until we lay them alongside the, ah, attack on Officer Gatling yesterday."

"We decided to call it a zorpse," Kyle called out.

"Pardon?"

"Well, Dr. Moreau refused to call it a zombie and animated corpse is just too much of a mouthful—"

"Hence zorpse," Kash finished from beside Kyle.

"I...see." Carrington cleared his throat, trying to regroup before he lost control of the meeting. "So, in order of occurrence, we have missing books concerning magic and necromancy from the Rare Books department at the library's main branch, plundered graves at Woodland Cemetery and a, for want of a better term, zorpse attack at the Walnut Lane Bridge. While we have no direct evidence to link these incidents, their timing strikes me as far too coincidental."

Audacity raised her paw.

"Yes, Cadet?"

She held up Jeff's drawing of the skull cufflink in her teeth.

"Yes, that's definitely part of the Woodland incident. Well done. That said, assignments as follows. Officer Gatling will handle Woodland from here. Find out from the Eighteenth who those graves belonged to, and anything else they might be willing to share. Officers

Wolf and Krisk, you'll be escorting our library consultant, Mr. Graham, to see Ms. Pecca Teecosi. He'll meet you in front of the library. Officer Virago, you're with them—no one should be out there in groups of less than three right now."

Vance called out in a voice that was trying for belligerent but trembled and cracked, "What about Jeff? I'm not leaving him here alone."

"I'm here, Virago," Lieutenant Dunfee said at her driest.

"Oh. Right. Yes, ma'am." Vance subsided, chastened. There would probably be no safer place in the city during a zombie attack than near Mia Dunfee.

Carrington glanced up to find LJ waving his sleeve frantically. "Yes, Mr. Jacket?"

LJ pointed to himself, rather emphatically, then pointed to Alex and Krisk at the back of the room.

"You haven't been to visit Ms. Teecosi yet?"

Somehow, LJ pulled in on himself enough to look sheepish as he twisted his shoulders in his version of shaking his head.

"Hmm. Perhaps it might pique her interest if you're there. By all means, go along." Carrington referred back to his notes. "Officer Soren, your contingent will be meeting with the head of Rare Books. Officers Dennis and Monroe with Officer Soren. The staff will show you where the books were housed. There may be traces of whatever happened to them. The library has not reported the books stolen quite yet, so do tread lightly, please. Officers Lourdes and Santos, check with the cemeteries within the city limits. Take Tim with you since he has a knack for finding small objects. Let's see if anyone else has anything odd to report."

"Why just in city limits?" Greg asked with a worried frown.

"Because if the worst case is true and we have some new plot brewing courtesy of our criminal mage, everything possibly connected has occurred in the city proper."

"And that's not ominous at all," Kyle muttered.

Amanda half-raised a hand. "Hey. Chopped liver over here?"

"You and I, Officer Zacchini, will take Officer Poole with us and return to the scene of the attack."

"I always tell my mom you take me to the nicest places."

That got the chuckles that Carrington couldn't have managed on his own and Amanda had timed her snark perfectly to the end of his spiel. *Well done, Manda*. He dismissed the troops and slouched back to his desk in relief. He'd done duty rosters for their shop for some time, yes, but there was something so *official* about ordering people and entities' specific activities for the day.

"You did good." Amanda patted him on the shoulder as she went past to secure her desk.

"Thank you. I'm uncertain why I was so nervous."

"'Cause you're usually the smartass half-asleep in the front row."

"I suppose that may have contributed."

Jeremy clattered up on the last word. "So what do I need to know, Sergeant?"

"You know that's not official yet." Carrington fought both eye roll and sigh. Some officers were just so...*young*. "We have no idea what we're dealing with yet, so stick close, stay alert and if I tell you to duck, dodge, dive for the ground or run like the devil himself is behind you, you do it."

Eyes wide, Jeremy nodded as if his neck were constructed of rubber bands. *Like those dreadful things they sell with the huge heads...* As was so often the case, the specific pop culture reference escaped Carrington.

He gave Jeff a sympathetic wave as they left the squad room, though he appeared content, 'porting an apple from desk to desk as he brought up files on his computer. Carrington stopped at the entrance to glance back and an odd shivery feeling washed over him at the image of Jeff alone and isolated from the rest of the squad. Prescient feelings weren't something Carrington experienced, at least he didn't believe so, but it was strong enough to stop him cold.

"Carr?" Amanda had a hand on his arm.

"It's...nothing." Carrington shook his head and kept walking. "Someone walking over my grave, I suppose."

"Seriously? You couldn't think of a different saying right now?"

"Heartfelt apologies." He gauged the sky — dotted here and there with gathering rainclouds — and slipped his sunglasses on before he stepped outside. Weather tended toward unsettled at this time of year and those clouds could decide to vanish at any moment.

They took nearly the same route as the previous day, parking in the Blue Bell Park lot and walking down the paths to the bridge this time rather than crashing through the trees. The shade was deep enough still despite the fallen leaves that Carrington could slip his sunglasses into his jacket pocket. Senses all on high alert, he strode ahead of his companions, following the zorpse trail. Not that this was difficult. A geriatric mastiff with severe allergies could have followed the scent.

He started at the point where Vance had brought the zorpse down and worked backward — along the path to the point of attack, through the scrub and clinging bushes where the thing had lurked. The fading scent trail led down to the water's edge.

"Jeremy?" Carrington pointed to a scrap of cloth snagged on a branch overhanging the Wissahickon. "Could you do a bit of careful levitation and retrieve that, please?"

"But—"

"Kyle says you've improved enormously. Just do your best."

Tongue protruding from the corner of his mouth, Jeremy took hold of the branch and rose a few inches from the ground. Rather than trusting his ability to direct his levitation, he proceeded hand-over-hand along the branch until he could retrieve the scrap.

*Sensible, at least. Our department can always use more sense.*

Jeremy tipped sideways in the air on his return journey, but Carrington and Amanda grabbed hold and reoriented him so he could land safely.

"Nicely done," Carrington murmured as he examined the cloth. "It's from our zorpse. The scent is unmistakable."

"I thought zombies couldn't cross water," Jeremy whispered.

"That's salt water." Carrington stared across the creek. "Traditionally, salt breaks the spell and allows the dead to rest. A better line of inquiry, Officer Poole, is what lies across the creek?"

"More park?"

"Hmm, yes. And beyond that?"

Jeremy pulled out his phone, tapping frantically. "There's a golf course. Couple steak places. Neighborhoods— Oh."

"Oh, what, kiddo?" Amanda prompted, though the set of her jaw said she knew.

"Leverington Cemetery." Jeremy swallowed hard.

Carrington gave a decisive nod. "Even so. The points of convenience multiply, wouldn't you say?"

Amanda drove them across the bridge to Leverington where, naturally, the sun decided to make its obnoxious and painful appearance as they climbed to the top of the hill. While shirking his duty wasn't an option, Carrington seriously considered asking the lieutenant if he might add an umbrella to his uniform.

It was a lovely cemetery with old trees, though vandals often targeted it, which sometimes lent the place a touch of melancholy. Prominently situated in the neighborhood atop the hill, it also had the odd feature of having a diner on the adjacent lot. *Though one has to remember the diner wasn't here back in the late eighteenth century. I wonder if the ghosts haunting here include the diner in their demesne. Do they stop in for ghost pie? Order ghost coffee to go on chilly mornings?*

Jeremy hurried his steps to walk on Carrington's left. "Isn't this a historic cemetery? Wasn't our, ah, guy from just a few decades ago?"

"It is historic, certainly. Some rather unique civil war monuments." Carrington pointed across the cemetery as they passed the wrought-iron fence with its granite entrance pillars. "That one is to a civil war nurse, Hetty Ann Jones. You can, perhaps, see the hospital tent carved into the side. But there are graves here from the nineteen eighties. Well within Dr. Moreau's guess of our ambulatory friend's age."

Carrington stood in the middle of the path—sun hammering down on him as his vampire instincts screamed at him to run for shadow—and sniffed. He turned several times, testing the air. "This way."

They wound their way around markers and monuments from three centuries, through well-kept stones and those that needed repair, through level graves and those that had suffered subsidence, until even a normal human nose could have followed the scent of freshly dug earth and decay.

The first disturbed graves had been largely empty with only bits broken off the coffins—a handle here, a decorative edging there. This grave still held its coffin, though the lid had been ripped off and hurled to the side. Of the occupant, there was no sign.

"Huh. There's skid marks here from the lid." Amanda bent over the furrows in the grass. "Lid skid isn't something I ever wanted to put in a report."

Jeremy let out a high, nervous giggle before clearing his throat.

"It may have been dragged," Carrington offered. "This is definitely our zorpse. The identical olfactory signature."

The granite marker, now sadly askew, read *Marlon Tum 1932-1987*, with no other inscription denoting he had been a beloved anything of anyone. Carrington found that rather sad.

"Are you picking up anything, Manda?"

Amanda dusted the dirt from her hands as she stood, shaking her head. "Nah. I'm getting a weird gray space here. I can see everything right in front of me, but if I look back, you know, into past stuff, it's like fog settled or something."

"Is it a similar feeling to attempting a post-cognitive image of the dust bunnies?"

"Kinda hard to say. They were gray and made their own weird fog. Maybe?" She shrugged. "Carr, I don't like this. It's all hinky."

"I have mentioned your absolute mastery of understatement, haven't I?" Carrington bent to scoop a sample of the grave dirt into an evidence bag, just in case. "I don't like it either, Manda. Reinforcements may be called for." He hefted the bag before sealing it and tucking it into his jacket. "This goes to the lieutenant. See if she perceives any residue of what happened here. Back to the shop for us."

\* \* \* \*

Erasmus gave up trying not to fidget as he waited on the library steps, waiting to be picked up by a police car driven by someone Carr had described in the past as a *virulent homophobe*. Though Carr also admitted that Officer Virago was trying to do better. And, oh, right, they'd be on their way to meet a powerful witch who lived in an invisible house.

*Nervous* didn't even scratch the surface of how he felt. He settled for twisting and untwisting the strap of his messenger bag so he wouldn't start yanking on his earlobe. When his black and white ride showed up, though, there were two cars. Alex drove the first one, with Krisk, of course, but also sleeves waving to him from the back window. He had to blink back his reaction and remind himself that the ghostly outerwear had names and they were Carrington's friends. Vance Virago drove the other car, alone.

Erasmus eased into the passenger seat with a wary nod. "Jeff's taking some time off?"

"Jeff's in the squad room," Vance growled as he pulled into traffic. A twitch of his shoulders seemed to settle him to some degree. "He's, um, not cleared for patrol yet."

*Is he all right* would have been the next obvious question, but Erasmus watched those big, scarred hands tremble against the steering wheel. "Are you all right?"

"Yeah, fine. *I* didn't — Fine."

That was the end of all conversation for the duration of the drive. Not the first time that morning, Erasmus wondered what had possessed Carrington to send this officer, out of all of them, to the Teecosi house. Certainly, he understood why Eva and Kash had gone to the library with Kyle. They were both sensitive to one degree or another and Kyle could enhance those abilities. But someone nonthreatening like Jeremy Poole would have been a better choice.

Maybe Carrington needed more sleep.

When they arrived at the apparently empty lot, Erasmus even managed to keep all the dumb sentences that wanted to pop out of his mouth to himself. *There's nothing here* and *how will we find an invisible house* were guaranteed to annoy his escort.

Alex let Hunter and LJ out of the back seat and made introductions, with Erasmus forewarned about how animated outerwear shook hands. Then they stood in a ragged line, staring at the weeds.

Vance leaned in and whispered, "Something supposed to happen?"

A soft rumble came from Alex's chest. "Thought she might see us out here. Guess she's busy." He cleared his throat and bellowed, "Pecca! Pecca Teecosi! Are you home?"

The only answer was the wind tugging mournfully at the corners of old fences. Erasmus expected a tumbleweed to roll by any second. When the line of light finally appeared, it was so unexpected that Erasmus took a step back. Perpendicular to the ground, the line grew wider until the vague outline of a door cracking open appeared.

"Officer Wolf-Who-Is-A-Human-Now?" a barely audible voice called from behind that door.

"It's me, Pecca. I have some —"

Alex didn't quite get to finish as a squeal cut him off. The door flung open to reveal an entrance hall inside, though there was still no outside house visible. A tall woman with a mass of auburn curls hurled herself down invisible steps and flung herself against Krisk's chest.

"Officer Lizard Person! You're all right!"

Krisk flicked his tongue a few times and gently set the woman, presumably Pecca, back as he nodded.

"I'm so glad. I haven't seen you since the hospital and you *weren't* all right then. That was terrible and I'm so sorry. But you look much better. And you've brought friends. Come in, come in. Has something happened?"

Erasmus exchanged a bemused glance with LJ — at least he thought he did — and followed their hostess inside. Pecca wasn't at all what he'd expected. Though the only experience he had of powerful magic workers was Auntie Mia, and maybe she wasn't a typical example. From the interior, the house was cozy, probably early twentieth century—and there was a patchwork dog jumping up on his leg.

"Patches! Down!" Pecca clicked her tongue at her cloth dog. "He likes you. You should be fine." She dismissed him to turn to Vance. "Firestarter. You will not hurt my friends or damage my house."

From everything he had heard, Erasmus braced for an obnoxious response, but Vance nodded, staring at the floor, and whispered, "Yes, ma'am. I mean...I wouldn't. How...?"

"I feel your fire. You need a better valve system." Pecca bent sideways, tipping her head to meet his eyes. "You can stay. It's safe here, you know."

He raised his head, uniform hat clutched in both hands. His gaze searched her still-tilted face and he nodded again.

"Pecca, this is LJ." Alex indicated the animated jacket who hung back behind Krisk. "The leather jacket I told you about."

"Ooooh. Come here, please. Let me touch you." Pecca held a hand out and waited for LJ to put his sleeve in her palm. "Yes, yes, this is Mama's magic." More cautiously than she had with Krisk, Pecca put her arms around LJ. "Welcome home, not-human brother."

LJ pulled his sleeve back and gesticulated some complex message.

"No, I don't remember you. Maybe you left right after she made you."

More sleeve and placket gesturing and nodding.

"Mama didn't always plan well when she made a new someone. I'm sorry. I wish I'd known you were out there lost and alone all that time."

LJ lifted sleeves and shoulders in a good approximation of a shrug, then turned and pointed to Hunter.

"And this is Hunter Green Pea Coat," Alex supplied. "She likes Hunter. And, um, she's LJ's coatfriend."

Head tilting to one side, then the other, Pecca's careful steps forward reminded Erasmus of a stalking crane. She touched Hunter's sleeve with two fingers and frowned. "You aren't Mama's. Do you remember being made?"

Trembling, Hunter bent her collar forward in a nod.

"And it scares you. Something slithers in the magic that made you. It's not nice."

Hunter yanked her sleeve back, though she didn't flee.

"It's not your fault. Don't ever think your making was your fault."

The nod was more hesitant this time, but Hunter's hem stopped trembling.

"So!" Pecca clapped her hands together, golden eyes bright as she turned to Alex. "I don't think you're here for just tea, Officer Wolf, but come back to the kitchen anyway and I'll make some. And you can tell me things."

Erasmus raised an eyebrow as she skipped down the hall in front of them. Definitely not what he'd expected. Pecca hurried about, her long skirt pooling and swirling about her brown legs and bare feet as she turned and flitted, putting on the kettle, gathering mugs and tea, and letting a group of wire butterflies land in her hair as if they were ornaments. She directed her bipedal guests to chairs and her non-pedal ones to perch on the counter. She even gave LJ and Hunter origami mugs so they wouldn't feel left out.

Too polite to barrel right into things, Alex waited until their hostess had settled with them, tea in front of everyone who could drink it, before he began. "Pecca, this is Erasmus Graham. He's a librarian."

Pecca turned to him with her unicorn mug clutched in both hands. "You are? Hmm. I would've thought something else. Never mind. Are you the reason everyone's visiting?"

"Partly, yes. Alex, do you want to start?"

Alex waved with his own mug, one with a prairie landscape, for Erasmus to go on.

"Well, there have been several incidents that the officers think might be connected. One has to do with the theft of books from the library." Erasmus turned to pull a folder out of his messenger bag and from that produced the list of books. "These are —"

"What were the others?" Pecca cut him off.

"The others?"

"Incidents. You said more than one. What were the others?"

Again, he looked to Alex for guidance and got a nod to keep the floor. "There... I don't have all the details, but there were graves disturbed. Dug up. The bodies missing. Then one of the officers was attacked —"

Pecca sat straighter as if she might bounce from her chair. "Is he all right?"

"I hope so," Vance muttered to his untouched tea.

"Is he your other half? I mean partner, since you're here without one and I don't think the librarian is. That would mean he's a police officer and not a librarian." Pecca leaned across Krisk to address Vance. "You could call him. Those unattached phones work in my house. We tried it before."

Vance startled, sloshing tea on the table.

"Maybe later then." Pecca reached across to stroke Vance's wrist. "Breathe, Officer Firestarter. And move slowly. I think Flap's going to land on your shoulder."

He stilled, watching out of the corner of his eye as a hand-sized origami crane fluttered down and perched on him. It seemed to give him a point of external focus so he wasn't staring into nothing any longer.

Erasmus waited until Pecca's attention returned to him before he slid the list of books across the table. "Right. Officer Gatling was attacked yesterday by what I'm told was an animated corpse. Because of the nature of the books that were stolen, our friends at the Seventy-Seventh think there's a connection. Are any of these titles familiar?"

"Yes." The word ended in a hiss as Pecca read down the list. "Twisted magic. Taking the lines and the flows and warping them. Black sorcery, the parts that mean anything at all. Men's magic."

"It can't be just men that do black magic, can it?" Erasmus asked, knowing the question could well be a powder keg.

"No. No, of course not." Pecca ran a finger down the list, bending close. "But women who did weren't so open about it. They knew better. Men could say it was research. Alchemy. Science. So they wrote it down. Women who weren't careful were burned. Women who practiced earth magic were burned. And many who had no magic at all."

"But...guys got executed too, right?" Vance blurted out.

She tipped her head side to side. "Yes, but it doesn't compare. And if you're thinking of that nonsense in Salem, that doesn't count. Nothing to do with magic." She flapped a hand as if shooing off a fly. "Never mind.

It's not important. But you should have been more careful with these books."

The way Pecca said it, her expression so serious with her curls falling into her face, somehow helped Erasmus not to bristle. "They were in a locked department in the library, in locked cabinets. It shouldn't have been possible for someone to take them."

"Did someone put holding spells on the locks, Mr. Librarian Conduit?"

Erasmus sat back as if she'd slapped him, and damn it, he was pulling on his ear again. "I don't... Ms. Teecosi, I can't work any magic and I don't understand what you mean."

Pecca picked her mug back up, sipping for a few moments. "No one to teach you. Such a shame for a powerful conduit. Not that you could cast the spell. You'd need a maker for that, but you could help."

"A maker." Erasmus stopped tugging his ear. "You're a maker, right?"

She gave him a bright smile and nodded encouragement.

"And you say I'm a conduit. How many types...roles are there in magic?"

The smile vanished and Pecca rose to scoop an animated kitty made of orange and yellow yarn pompoms from the floor. She petted the textile cat as she stared out of the window, though Erasmus couldn't say whether she was thinking or ignoring his question.

Finally, she murmured to the kitty, "They're in trouble, Fluff, aren't they? The whole city might be. They need so many more things than they know."

"Ms. Pecca?" Alex spoke up with the throat clearing he often did to alleviate some of the growl in his voice.

"I think we're in trouble, too. Anything you can tell us will help. Even if it's just about how magic works."

"I don't want anything to happen to you or Officer Lizard Person." Pecca heaved a shuddering breath. "I promised Mama I would never teach anyone unless they were the next one after me. But this is different. There's someone so, so bad out there."

Again she stopped, but only long enough to put the yarn kitty down and return to the table. "I wish I had years. There's enough here to meet any black sorcerer. But I don't think he'll give us years. Not from what you told me. Magic…is. It's in everything. A part of everything. Runs through our lives and our world in eddies and streams. Lives in all of us."

Krisk's tail thumped the kitchen floor as he typed on his phone. He held it out to Pecca to read.

"Not quite. Not every human can learn to work magic. Some are, well, most are…like they're wrapped in cellophane. They might know it's out there, but they can't touch it." Pecca picked up her cooling tea and sipped. "Some humans can even learn every aspect of magic. They can be good and helpful or they can be very, very dangerous. Most humans just get one thing, though. Mr. Librarian, you're a conduit. A high-flow one, I can feel it. You can *pull* power, but you can't do anything with it. Officer Wolf is a source. He's a place where power pools, but that's all. Officer Firestarter —"

"Vance," the officer in question interrupted on a sharp intake of breath.

"Vance," Pecca repeated. "It's a good name. You could be a maker. If someone had taught you."

The firestarter's face had turned a shade to match his talent. Erasmus wondered if actual steam would creep out under his collar if he turned any redder. Vance mumbled something and hid his confusion in gulping down tea.

"What was Captain Vampire, Pecca?" Alex asked.

"Oh, he's all three, but not taught very well. He probably wouldn't like to hear that, would he?"

Alex's lips compressed as if he were forcing back a smile. "Probably not. Never saw him make anything, though."

"There's making and there's making." Pecca held out an arm and the origami crane fluttered to her. "I *made* Flap and Fluff and Patches, just like Mama made LJ. But maker means spells, which don't always *make* things."

"I see. Making spells." Erasmus took his notebook out and started scribbling down the new vocabulary. "Source, conduit, maker. Sometimes all three in one person, which would make them more powerful, wouldn't it? They would have power to pull and direct and shape."

"They would, if they had a teacher or studied hard." Pecca waved a hand to Erasmus' list.

"You think this sorcerer, the one who's animating bodies...you think he's one of these all three people, don't you?"

Pecca nodded, eyes huge in a solemn face.

Putting his teacup down with great care, as if he might miss the table, Alex said, "I think we're gonna need to talk to Carr about reinforcements."

# Chapter Four

A quiet squad room could be soothing or it could grate on a vampire's nerves. This near-silence, with the few officers present all withdrawn into themselves and trying to slog through paperwork while they waited for the other teams to straggle in? A bone-itching level of aggravation.

Even Larry the ghost had picked up on the strained atmosphere and had ceased his whistling as he poured out the untouched terrible coffee and made a fresh pot without a sound. Audacity had retreated under her dad's desk for a kitten-nap. Edgar sulked on his perch, neon pink and blue feathers fluffed up until he looked like a discarded ball of cotton candy. Jeff had nothing to report since he was waiting for a call back from the Eighteenth.

Carrington had given the grave dirt to Lieutenant Dunfee, her frown several degrees more forbidding than usual as she took the bag gingerly between thumb and forefinger. With that one duty discharged, he had nothing that he cared to work on. Unlike most of his colleagues, he was meticulous to the point of neurosis about keeping up with paperwork.

"Manda, talk to me. Please."

"'Bout what?" Amanda's voice on the other side of the monitors sounded muffled, as if she were looking under her desk.

"Anything."

"Flyers play tonight. I'm really liking —"

"Anything but professional sports."

Amanda's snort was quite clear, so she must have found whatever it was. "Damn picky vamp. I could tell you the story about my brother and the falafel vendor again."

"That *is* a good story."

"Okay, so it was raining —"

A louder-than-usual commotion from officers coming through the front door interrupted the tale. Not a tragedy, since Carrington had certainly heard it before, but it did sound like too *many* people. He rose from his chair slump to go find the answer to the question, *what in blazes?*

As people and entities came in from the hallway, it became clear that there was only one extra person, but everyone was talking over each other. They stopped at the far end of the squad room as Edgar came out of his dozing sulk, flapping his wings and crying out, "Rrrrraaak! Invader witch! Invader witch!"

Audacity careened around the desks to put herself in front of Carrington, growling, feet planted, as if she had to protect him.

"Stand down, Cadet," Carrington ordered for her ears only, then with more volume, "You too, Edgar.

She's hardly an invader. She's holding LJ's and Hunter's hands. Er, sleeves."

"Rrrrr." Edgar re-fluffed in irritation. "Fucking civilians."

Carrington picked up Audacity and approached the mob, Kash's contingent on one side, Alex's on the other, with LJ, Hunter and a tall auburn-haired woman between them. He had to look up a smidge when he stopped before her.

"Good afternoon. Please excuse the raven. He's incorrigible. I'm Officer Loveless." Carrington held the hand out that wasn't currently supporting kitten. "And I have to assume you're Ms. Pecca Teecosi."

The woman released both coat sleeves and put her hands up to her cheeks. "You are the most adorable little vampire I've ever seen. Oh! If you'd come to my door, I might have let you in even without Officer Wolf-Who-Was-A-Wolf."

"Ah, thank you. I think." Carrington dropped the hand that was obviously not going to be shaken and turned to his officers. "Explanations? Reports?"

No immediate answers were forthcoming since all of his officers were busy trying to choke back bouts of stifled laughter. LJ was doubled over, slapping a nonexistent knee, while Hunter had both sleeves up over her nonexistent mouth. Only his wonderful Erasmus wasn't laughing.

"You're not little. You're taller than I am," he said with a soft smile. "I'd guess Ms. Pecca's only seen vampires as tall as that vampire captain who comes to visit."

"Lovely. So even in this, I fall short." *That* only set the hilarity off again and Carrington rolled his eyes, waiting for his officers to recover their various dignities. "So. Officer Soren? Anything from the library?"

Kash managed a straight face, though little hitches still crept into his speech. "Not too much to tell. The cases were tampered with. Magic residue on the locks. Eva..." Kash turned to Officer Dennis, all traces of mirth gone. "Says it was dark."

"You could read a cabinet's aura?" Carrington refrained from scratching his head.

"It wasn't... It was different from a person's aura." Eva shrugged. "But with Kyle helping, I could see *something* was there. It felt slimy and heavy, like it was trying to suck the light out of the room."

"At least we know what happened to the books." Erasmus rubbed at his temples. "It doesn't make me *happy*, but at least we know."

"We'll do our best to recover them." Carrington's arms ached to hold him, to rub his back and ease some of the obvious tension. *But not while in a professional capacity.* "What has your expedition turned up? Aside from Ms. Teecosi."

Erasmus let out one of those warm chuckles that made Carrington's insides melt. "Ms. Teecosi *is* what we turned up. We've been discussing magic, and how powerful this person is, if it's the same person who's been causing havoc for you."

Pecca stepped forward and startled Carrington by placing both hands on his shoulders. "Source."

"What—" Carrington tried to ask but Erasmus gave a little wave of discouragement. He was taking notes, of all things.

Circling around to Jeremy, she put a finger under his chin to lift his face. "Conduit." Then on to Amanda, whose arm she took. "Source. Nearly as strong as

Officer Vampire." She pointed to Greg and Shira when they hurried in from the front hall. "Both conduits." Peering into Kyle's eyes for the longest time, she said softly, "You know what you are. But your conduit isn't some plain, simple piece of kitchen pipe."

Kyle gaped at her before he managed, "Yeah, I guess I'm kinda twisted."

This went on until she had given everyone, including Edgar, who was a source, a designation of either source, conduit or maker. The last seemed the most unusual since she only named Kash and Vance as makers.

Carrington forced his eyebrows back down to their normal places. "I'm very much hoping someone will explain."

In a swirl of skirts and bell sleeves, Pecca was in front of him again, her steps more like a dance than walking. And was she…barefoot? "This sorcerer. The one who tricked me. The one who makes abominations and pulls the dead from their rest, he is powerful and knows so much and now he has all those horrible books. And you need help."

"Ms. Teecosi, how do you know anything about him at all?" Carrington thought of fairies when he watched her, fairies and birds, as if she might sprout wings at any moment. She smelled human, but how would he know? There weren't any fae around to smell.

"Makers these days…" She swept a hand to include the squad. "They're around. But not like before. No one gets taught. The ones that do things, really, truly *do* — they're rare. One like this, that can make horrible things and throw confusion around himself? There can't be more than one."

"I'll grant that for now. But you've lived in isolation so long. Why come out to help us after all this time?"

Pecca leaned in, their noses nearly touching, and Carrington's eyes began to cross. "He looked through me, Officer Vampire. Knew what I could do and what I wanted most. He knew and he *used* me. I didn't like that one bit."

"More than fair." Carrington nodded and took a step back to ease the strain on his eyes. "But I don't understand to what purpose you've given us all…these designations."

"It's how we all process magic, for want of a better word," Erasmus said. "How we naturally react to it."

"Older worldview, not shared by State." Lieutenant Dunfee's sharp voice made Carrington twitch and spin toward her office. She stood by her door with Edgar on her shoulder. "At least never officially and teaching officers outside of headquarters isn't something I can officially condone."

*Officially.* Carrington heard the subtext there. "How did you learn, ma'am?"

"From my mother, as Ms. Teecosi did." The lieutenant met his gaze and held it. "Valbuena will have to be told."

"Yes, ma'am. Of course."

She stared a moment longer, then pointed to Pecca with her chin. "Her talents are broader than mine. More free-range, in a way, and more powerful. Edgar can feel it from here. Learn all you can, while you can, but you'll have to do it off duty. I don't know what's coming. I do know it's going to be bad." She fed Edgar a treat from her jacket pocket. "Carry on, officers, entities, Mr. Graham. Don't make a mess of my squad room, Ms. Teecosi."

With that, she strode back to her office and closed the door.

"We'll need her," Pecca whispered to Alex. "She's very powerful, too."

"Pretty sure she'll be there if we do," Alex told her at the same volume. "The lieutenant...well, she knows stuff."

Carrington turned to Erasmus and held both hands up in supplication. "I still am waiting, ever so patiently, for an explanation."

Finally, his librarian laid everything out, defining the terms and detailing what role Pecca proposed to play in the storm that everyone seemed to know was gathering.

"Ms. Pecca believes a confrontation with the sorcerer is inevitable. That whatever he's planning won't be something subtle and isolated, and while there isn't time to teach anyone properly, we need to be more ready than we are now."

"We?" Carrington lost control of his eyebrows again.

"I'm part of this too, Carr."

Carrington pinched the bridge of his nose between thumb and forefinger, keeping a tight rein on his rising fear. "Could we discuss this later, please? Without an audience."

Erasmus squinted at him, a stubborn set to his jaw, but at least he nodded at the part about not having it out in public.

Toward the back of the room, Pecca had crouched down to talk to Audacity, who danced forward a couple of steps before racing back out of reach, obviously uncertain. Her dad thought Pecca was acceptable, so their cadet familiar would get there.

Everyone else had drifted toward them, leaving Erasmus and Carrington in an odd puddle of quiet.

"All right." Ras' expression had relaxed, indicating he'd put away personal things to deal with the matter at hand. *One of the reasons I love him so.* "So you're a source, which means you gather and store magic, like a reservoir. A conduit would be able to pull magic from you and from magic in their surroundings, but unless the conduit knows how to manipulate magic, it wouldn't do them much good. A maker *does* manipulate, as Vance does when he conjures and controls flame. As Kash does when he directs magic as a physical force. A maker can pull directly from a source for powerful workings, but from what Pecca says, a conduit in between amplifies it."

"Ah. So Kyle, as a natural untrained conduit with some odd wiring, was always doing as his construction dictates. More or less."

"We need to stay away from the mixed construction metaphors." Ras gave him a wry smile. "But essentially, yes. Also, need to mention that Pecca verified LJ as one of her mother's creations. Hunter isn't. Not only that—Hunter's creator frightens her."

An avalanche of suspicions tumbled into Carrington's forebrain. Hunter had appeared during the book incident. Hunter had understood how to contain the attack books. Hunter had been here while this mage—this sorcerer—seemed to have more and more intelligence regarding the squad's movements. *Hunter*—

"Carr, stop. Your jaw is ticking. I know where you're going since I thought of that, too. But don't go there without knowing."

"I would never…" Except he had been. "No. You're right. A confrontation would be counterproductive either way."

Carrington pulled the evidence bag with the scrap of cloth from his jacket pocket and pulled Hunter into the quieter part of the squad room. She bobbed as she floated, wringing her sleeves, something in his manner obviously making her nervous.

"I'd like you to take a look at this for me. I know you've picked up bits of magic before and I want to know if you recognize it."

Hunter did a slow collar nod. When Carrington offered the opened bag to her, she reached a sleeve in. The moment she connected with the zorpse cloth, Hunter jerked her sleeve back, shaking. She waved one cuff over the other in frantic negation and fled toward the back of the station.

"That went well," Ras said in his driest tone.

"Hush. I'm not giving up quite yet." Carrington snagged a pen and legal pad from his desk and strode toward the room LJ and Hunter shared. He caught LJ trying to follow him out of the corner of his eye, but Erasmus stopped him with a hand on his front placket and a quiet word.

Carrington closed the door and sat on the bed. "Hunter, I know you're in here. No matter what's happened, no matter what you believe has happened, no one here will hurt you."

Rustling came from under the bed, but Hunter didn't poke so much as a button out.

"I'll be candid. You and I both know that this criminal sorcerer might have made you. Maybe you think that I think that you've been set here as a mole, a spy, and that you think I mean you harm because of it. That was far too much thinking in one sentence. I have a pad and pen. Would much rather hear, er, see your side of the story than drawing false conclusions."

A sliver of collar peeked out from under the bed frame, then a little more.

"I'm sitting here peacefully and vow to keep my hands to myself. Please, Hunter. Talk to me."

She slid out bit by bit and floated up to settle at the head of the bed, as far away from Carrington as she could manage. With exaggerated care, he set the pad and pen on the bed and slid both toward her.

When she took them, slowly, her attention never wavering from Carrington, he finally asked, "So I assume something about the lingering magic on that piece of cloth reminds you of your creator."

She gave a slow nod.

"Do you know what he looks like?"

After another long hesitation, Hunter began to draw. She turned the pad around to show Carrington a picture of eyes with the word *no* underneath, and a picture of a hand touching a flat surface with the word *yes*.

"You don't know what he looks like but you know the feel of him?" At her nod, Carrington went on, "Would you need to be right next to him to know him, would you think?"

Her shrug seemed weary, defeated, not at all like Hunter.

"All right, we'll leave possible identification aside for now. Do you recall anything about when you were created? Were you there long, in whatever place it was?"

The next picture she showed him was her coatself fleeing.

"I see. You ran as soon as you could. I can't blame you in the least. Do you recall anything about the place? Was it a house? An old factory?"

This time she drew furiously and turned a more elaborate picture toward him. This one was of a house with many windows and several trees that appeared small in comparison.

"It was a big house," Carrington guessed. "A house someone wealthy would own." At her nod, a terrible realization crept over him. "The day of the reception here—you were sure your creator would be on the guest list. All those wealthy society names."

Again, she nodded.

"But you can't be sure because you wouldn't come out."

Hunter hunched in on herself, nodding disconsolately.

"Please don't feel guilty about that." Carrington dared to lean forward, hands clasped between his knees. "You were frightened and had every reason to be. I need to ask you two more things."

Pad and pen went on the bed as Hunter gave a more definite nod.

"If you were somehow being coerced or threatened into providing information, I need you to know that we *will* protect you." Carrington watched her carefully, but she remained still, perhaps waiting for an accusation. "Are you?"

She crossed her sleeves in front of her in an obvious gesture of offense and twisted her collar back and forth in a definite *no*.

"Do you think, perhaps, there is some way your creator is using you for information? That there's some connection still there that you might not be entirely aware of?"

Hunter lifter both sleeves in a more elaborate shrug.

"All right. My apologies for the interrogation." Carrington stood and offered an arm. "It might be best if we rejoined the others before LJ has several conniptions."

The little bit of shaking with one cuff up where her mouth would have been was probably a snicker. She took his arm as if Carrington were about to escort her to a gala and they ambled back to the squad room where LJ accosted them, sleeves flying in wild gesticulations, pointing in accusation at Carrington. Hunter swatted at her coatfriend and patted Carrington's arm, the meaning obvious. *Stop it. He's our friend.*

Carrington left her talking to LJ and clapped his hands together sharply as he returned to the center of the desks. "Well then. Let's see what we know. Officer Poole, what do you have for us on our Leverington zorpse, Marlon Tum?"

"Me? Oh…" Jeremy stood up from his desk as if he were going to recite, shuffled his feet and sat back down before he read from his screen. "Obituary from the archives states that Marlon Tum was an actor who died on stage during a performance of *Macbeth* —"

"Thus furthering the reputation of *The Scottish Play*," Carrington murmured. "Anything else?"

"It doesn't list any surviving relatives and the cause of death was a stroke. Poor guy didn't have anyone to write anything nice about him, I guess."

"An actor?" Shira leaned around Jeff to address Carrington.

"That has the sound of a beginning to it." Carrington waved her forward. "What did you and Officer Santos uncover, if you'll pardon the pun."

"We uncovered actors." Shira pulled her notepad from her desk. "Atticus Rohmer, died nineteen sixty-two. An actor with the *Orphée* Company until he died of a fall from the scaffolding. Clara Nippert, died nineteen seventy-five. An actress with various local companies who died of a sudden heart attack in the wings while waiting for her cue." She glanced up. "Those are your two from Woodland, Carr."

"There's seven more, never more than one or two graves dug up in any one cemetery," Greg added. "We haven't been able to run down all the obits yet, but anyone wanna take bets they're all actors?"

Kyle held up both hands. "*Not* taking that bet. But why the hell just actors for a thing of zombies?" He turned to his husband. "What's the collective noun for zombies?"

"Why would I know that?" Kash turned his gaze ceilingward. "Why would *anyone* know that?"

"I'll take horror genre collective nouns for a hundred, please," Jeff said with a poorly concealed snicker. "I think horde works."

Pecca raised a hand, waving it wildly. "Oh! Shambles! I like shambles for a group of zombies. This is fun. Is this how investigations usually work?"

"Ah, perhaps not so much in other departments." Carrington allowed a hint of a smile for her. "We're more collaborative here. And since you're here and we have your expertise—Hunter and I spoke, and we agree there's a chance that she was not only created by this criminal mage, though she doesn't remember where, but also that she might still be inadvertently connected to him. Is there a way to verify?"

"Yes, yes, of course. Easy-peasy."

"Could you…?"

"But I need things. And time. Not quite as easy as making tea. Though even then, you still need tea."

"Truer words, Ms. Pecca. One still needs tea." Carrington drummed his fingers on his forearm, trying to dredge up next steps, and went right back to addressing Pecca. "Am I correct in assuming Officers Soren and Virago pack the most power out of all of our officers, magically speaking?"

Pecca cocked her head to one side, more birdlike than ever. "In a way, yes."

"Would you like to start the teaching with them? After shift, perhaps?"

"It can't just be them." Pecca whirled and pointed to Amanda, Shira, Eva and Kyle. "You, you, you and most especially you. All together or it's all unconnected nonsense."

Vance blurted out, "But Jeff—"

"Will be next." Pecca floated to him and took his hands, apparently unaware that Vance had turned so red, Carrington wondered if he might have a stroke. "You need to learn to work with any conduit. In a bad spot, the most familiar might not be nearest."

An incoherent, strangled sound escaped Vance, not unlike the call of a moose drowning in quicksand, but he managed a rapid-fire nod.

"Come to my street when you're ready tonight. I'll make soup." Pecca began to flitter her way out of the squad room.

"Ms. Pecca?" Alex called after her. "Don't you want me to take you home?"

"No need," she called back with an airy wave.

"Oh. Do you fly or something?"

Her voice floated back from the front hall. "No, I take the bus."

After a stunned moment of silence, Kash said, "Interesting person. She *is* a person?"

"Smells human to me," Alex offered. "Carr?"

"Yes. She's unusual. Perhaps not like us, but undeniably human."

"What's up, Vance?" Kyle called out to the still-blinking firestarter. "You afraid of her?"

Vance went from distracted blinking to instant scowl. "Shut the fuck up. No."

Before that could escalate, Carrington put the squad to work searching for the obits from the rest of the plundered graves and asked Vance to help Erasmus compile a list of intersecting contents from the stolen books. He and Ras both knew what they would find, but maybe some hint would emerge from the exercise as to what this sorcerer — this *necromancer* intended. Was Vance frightened of Pecca? Carrington snorted to himself. Probably not in the way Kyle implied and if Vance wasn't completely twitterpated, Carrington would eat his keyboard.

* * * *

Erasmus picked up the menu, though he knew it by heart. The little diner-coffee shop nearest Carr's apartment was a favorite fallback when they'd both had a rough day. Carrington slouched in the seat across, his head resting on the back of his chair, while Jeff had the chair beside him, occupied with considerably more grace.

"Let's move to Martinique," Carrington said without bothering to open his eyes.

"Why there all of a sudden?"

"I want a quiet, provincial life."

Jeff chuckled softly. "Carrington Loveless III — anti-Belle."

"Hilarious."

Usually, they'd have Amanda with them instead of Jeff, but Jeff had mentioned not knowing what to do for dinner and Pecca had stolen Amanda. Besides, Erasmus liked what he'd seen of Jeff. He was hard to pin down socially, someone who never seemed to have a girlfriend or boyfriend, but was sociable, funny, good-looking in a cop sort of way and an excellent listener. He was eminently dateable, but Erasmus suspected he might not be interested.

Carrington patted Jeff's arm. "So. You're doing all right? Truly?"

"I'm okay." Even though Jeff said it, a visible shudder ran through him. "Might have to sleep with a nightlight on for a while."

Erasmus put the menu back in its metal holder. "Does anyone live with you?"

"I'm the only human in my apartment, but I'm not exactly alone." Jeff gave him that wry smile. "I have two cats and a ferret who thinks she's a cat. As long as they're not upset, I know everything's fine. It's the Jonesy phenomenon."

"Of course." Erasmus offered a serious nod. "Cats are happy, no alien monster."

"Or zorpses." Carrington sat up from his sprawl. "Speaking of which, Ras, this is an absurdly dangerous case."

*I know where this is going*. He received a short reprieve as the waitress came to take his order and Jeff's. She was one of the regulars who didn't even ask if Carrington was ordering any more and just brought him a full pitcher of ice water.

When she walked off again, Erasmus leaned across the table and took Carrington's hand. "You're going to tell me that this case is no place for a civilian. That it's too dangerous and I shouldn't involve myself."

"Yes. Quite sensible of you." Carrington's frown indicated that he didn't at all mean what he said.

"Be right back. Restroom stop." Jeff took the diplomatic route and left them the table for a few moments.

"I'm already involved, Carr. I've been attacked twice by this sorcerer. I have a limp that'll probably always be with me from the last time." Low blow, he knew that, and a stone of guilt settled in his stomach at Carrington's wince. "Those books are from my department, too. So we've provided the tools he needs to do whatever this is."

Carrington's expression twisted, a distinct glisten in his eyes. "I can't see you hurt again. The last time very nearly killed me. Ras...I can't."

"Do you think it's so much different for me when I let you walk out the door every morning? A little bit of me dies, wondering if today's the day something happens. I try not to dwell on it too much, but that bit's there until you're home again."

"I'm a *vampire*. Nearly indestructible. It's not the same thing at all."

"The key word here is *nearly*. You're not made of titanium, Carr. Besides, I know better than to jump into a firefight. I'm not saying that. But let me be prepared.

Let me learn how to be useful in a bad spot. Don't shut me out. I'm already in this past my waders."

Carrington leaned his forehead atop their joined hands. "I can't. Ras—"

They were interrupted again by the delivery of curly fries and Carrington pulled his hand back, swiping at his eyes.

"I didn't mean to upset you, hon. I'm sorry. Why don't you have your dinner and we'll pick this up later."

"Yes. Of course." Carrington heaved a long breath and attempted a smile as he pulled his thermos out of his bag. "Between being tired and hungry, I'm probably a bit past emotional."

When Jeff returned, they were both steadier, with Carrington complaining about the messages his mother kept leaving.

"She could state a purpose to her call instead of leaving such vague phrases about needing to speak to me and me never picking up my phone. I refuse to be guilted into returning her call tonight."

"Parents are great." Jeff halted his meticulous predation of curly fries. "Mine keep bugging me to come see them at their new place."

Erasmus tilted his head in puzzlement. "I don't mean to pry, but why haven't you?"

"I'd be happy to, and I will when I get some time off, but they moved to the beach. All the way down in Lewes and you know what *that* drive's like on the weekends."

Dinner came out soon after, a pulled pork sandwich for Jeff and a Reuben for Erasmus, and the rest of the meal passed in quiet conversation about families and school experiences. There was less teasing without

Amanda there, but this seemed to Erasmus to be something all three of them needed—a few quiet, normal moments.

"We'll walk you to your car," Carrington said as they pushed back from the table.

"I appreciate the thought, but you don't have to do that." Jeff raised an eyebrow at Carrington. "I'm a big boy, Carr, and a police officer, in case you forgot."

Erasmus patted his arm. "No one forgot. Let us walk with you so Carrington doesn't worry. Please, please don't make him start fretting just before we go home."

Jeff laughed and shook his head. "For Carr's peace of mind and you not murdering him out of aggravation, okay."

The crisp autumn air hit them as they left the warm confines of the diner—the sort of clean chill that reminded Erasmus of caramel apples and sweet potato pies. He realized he'd never talked about Carrington's approach to Halloween. Would he allow trick-or-treaters? Though maybe Halloween at Erasmus' moms' house would be better. More kids than they'd get at Carrington's condo.

As they turned the corner and came in sight of Jeff's car—which he'd parked toward the Fairmount end of Kelly Drive—Erasmus started to wish for gloves. Crisp was fine, but out here closer to the river the wind had teeth. The shrubs on their left rustled and Erasmus sidled away from them in startled caution. *Wind, you ninny. It's just wind.* Though he didn't miss Carrington stopping to sniff the air.

As soon as he'd thought it, the rustling became crashing through branches. A hideous wet growl wove amid the bushes as a body lurched free of the shrubbery. Quite literally a body, with empty eye sockets and strings of flesh hanging between the remains of a moldering suit.

"Ras!" Carrington yanked Erasmus behind him just as bony fingers scraped his wrist.

The walking corpse moaned, jaw creaking as it formed barely distinct words. "Yes, I have tricks in my pocket, I have things up my sleeve. But I am the opposite of a stage magician. He gives you illusion that has the appearance of truth."

"*Glass Menagerie!*" Erasmus shouted, as if naming the play from which the lines came could hold off the undead.

The thing's foul smell made him gag and he had no idea how Carrington could bear to face it. Carrington took a swipe at it, but it shambled past, reaching for Jeff, who cried out and stumbled back, pulling his weapon.

"Not again," Carrington snarled and launched himself at the zorpse. "No brains for you!"

He hit with a sickening thud and both vampire and undead actor fell to the sidewalk in a series of snaps and crunches. Carrington took the thing by the skull and wrenched its head from its neck while the thing tried to wrap partially decomposed fingers around his throat. The head came free with a horrible creak and snap, and Carrington flung it toward the shrubbery.

Decapitation seemed a good solution though. After a few twitches, the zorpse collapsed and lay still.

"Hell and thunder!" Carrington surged up from his crouch, wiping fretfully at his arms. "That was revolting. Everyone all right?"

"Sweet Jesus." Jeff sank to his knees, rubbing at his chest. "No problem. I didn't need my heart."

"Fine." Erasmus clamped his jaw, trying to stop his shuddering. "I'm fine."

Carrington stripped off his jacket and dropped it to the sidewalk before he strode over to envelope Erasmus in a hard hug. "I'm sorry, sweetheart. I'm so sorry. No excuse for being distracted right now, but I heard it a second too late. You're certain you're all right?"

"Really, I'm fine." Erasmus still laid his head on Carrington's shoulder, steadying himself on his vampire's unfailing courage and strength. "It barely touched me."

"Good, good. I need to call this in. Get this thing off the street."

"Already on it, Carr," Jeff called from where he sat on the pavement. "I'd feel better if your ears are free to listen for any more of them."

"Excellent point." Carrington lifted his head, taking on the aspect of a wolf casting about for prey, but he didn't remove his arms from around Erasmus, for which he was profoundly, embarrassingly glad.

An hour and a half later, with the zorpse carted off to Dr. Moreau, Jeff seen to his car, and Carrington's clothes in the washing machine, Erasmus finally felt as if his insides had stopped quivering. It wasn't that the zorpse had been particularly powerful or dangerous — Carrington had dealt with it without any strain — but it had been the shock. That was what he told himself, at least.

"Shouldn't you call your mother?"

Carrington responded by shoving his head under a sofa cushion. "No, no and again, no. I'm not dealing with her tonight. Have pity."

"I guess I can find a little pity. But don't forget about it tomorrow when I'm not there to nag you. What if it's something important?"

"If it were something vital, she would have left a message. Like the terse *your father's in the hospital* when Dad had his heart attack."

"I see." Erasmus pulled the pillow away, since it disturbed him to see Carrington looking headless, and plunked down on the sofa beside him. "I'm going to have nightmares forever. But why actors, do you think?"

"Was it really from Tennessee Williams? What the zorpse said?" Carrington sat up and opened his arms for Erasmus to snuggle into.

"It was. I remember that scene."

"I don't know, my dear. I really haven't the first notion. If this necromancer only uses deceased actors, it could be some characteristic that they share or it could even be an aesthetic choice for all I know."

"Are there aesthetics in necromancy?"

"Suppose there could be. Classical necromancy, where one only resurrects corpses with crisp, clean lines. Rococo necromancy, which picks corpses who have extra decorative bits. Gothic necromancy —"

"That sounds sort of redundant."

"Well, yes, but a proper Gothic necromancer would only choose the corpses with the darkest, most tortured pasts."

Erasmus managed a snicker since Carrington had said it all in such a serious, stuffy tone. "I feel like my degrees were lacking in necromantic studies."

"Shame, that. Schools don't teach the classics like they used to."

"Carr? I hate to suggest this, but did it look like that thing was after Jeff?"

Carrington nodded against the top of his head. "I'm not jumping to conclusions, but it's something we have to take note of. And to guard against."

"Do you think he's all right going home? Since no one's there?"

"I'm more concerned about him getting to and from. But once he's home, he has cats."

That statement, spoken without a trace of irony, illustrated to Erasmus just how far down the rabbit hole he'd fallen, and it wasn't one of Ms. Potter's rabbit's either.

* * * *

"Are you sure you still have time?" Phone tucked between chin and shoulder, Erasmus secured his computer and locked up his desk for lunchtime. He'd promised to come over to his moms' for an early lunch and Carrington had been pleased to be asked along, but that had been before the first zorpse incident.

"I don't have anything pressing right now," Carrington assured him. "State Paranormal's been informed of recent developments. I don't have any other cases outstanding, so I'm at your disposal."

Tasha Graham, his biological mother, and Roshanda Wilkes, his other mom, had one of the cozy, older brownstones in the Graduate Hospital neighborhood. They'd bought it years before the prices had started to climb in that part of town, and while it had been a little tight when Erasmus and both of his sisters were still at home, now it was the perfect house for two. Not that it ever felt empty, since both extended families lived close by and someone was always visiting.

Both had worked for the city years ago, but they'd left the public sector to work independently—Tasha as a much sought-after editor of genre fiction, while Roshanda ran a small, efficient private security company.

Erasmus made his way down the street from the bus stop, just as Carrington reached the brownstone's front steps from the other direction.

"Problems parking?" Erasmus called out.

"Not too much." Carrington waved behind him. "Just a block down."

Before they had a chance to knock, Mom opened the door with a huge smile. "There you both are. Get in here before lunch gets cold."

Carrington still appeared bemused by the huge hugs he always received from both Mom and Mom Shanda, but he hugged back as if parental affection were water in the desert. Heavenly scents of beef stew and fresh bread threaded through the house, and it was all Erasmus could do to hang his coat up politely and walk, not run, toward the kitchen.

"Grab a bowl and serve yourself." Mom waved a hand at the stove. "Carrington, there's tea in the fridge if you want some. No sugar. How've you been? How's your family?"

"Everyone's fine, ma'am. Their usual selves," Carrington said with a shy smile as he reached into the cabinet for a glass.

"One of these days, I'll get you to stop calling me ma'am." Mom gave him a fierce scowl, though her eyes twinkled. "Come sit. Tell us what's been happening."

The stew was wonderful, as always, with big chunks of carrots and potatoes. Erasmus could have died for the homemade bread, so he tried to be polite and talk between mouthfuls, but he knew he wasn't doing a great job.

"I told you about the missing books, didn't I?"

Mom Shanda nodded. "You did. I still say they were stolen."

"Yeah, I was hoping they weren't. But Carr sent people over, people who could tell certain things, and you were right. Someone not only stole old books of dangerous magic, they used magic to do it. Carr thinks it's the same person who made the word-spitting books and the carnivorous dust bunnies."

"That right?" Mom Shanda pinned Carrington with a hard stare. "Any idea who this dangerous person is?"

"Ah, hmm." Carrington took a long drink of ice tea. "We're working on it. We have reason — several reasons — to believe this magic user, sorcerer, whatever we want to call him, has been watching the precinct for a long time now."

"Watching?" Mom Shanda broke off a piece of her bread to butter it. "You mean targeting?"

"It's an uncomfortable word, but I won't deny it. Especially now, with new developments."

Mom looked from Erasmus to Carrington with a worried frown. "What developments?"

They took it in turns, relating the details of the zorpse attacks, with Carrington stopping to explain why they were called zorpses and the strange phenomenon of the ones they'd encountered so far spouting lines from plays.

"Salt," Mom said when they'd reached the end. "Shouldn't salt take care of them?"

"This isn't the same kind of zombie." Mom Shanda's tone was even more serious than normal. "The *bokor*, the voodoo sorcerer, he'd use people who'd just died.

Sometimes suicides. Sometimes he'd kill them himself. Those zombie slaves, tied to the *bokor*, you could give them something salted to eat and they'd be freed to rest in peace. This...however this practitioner's done it, this isn't a voodoo practice, raising people who've been long dead. Ripping them from the other side and forcing them back into rotten remains."

"They should still have salt," Mom insisted. "What kind of paranormal investigators wander around without salt?"

"It's not standard issue." Carrington hesitated with a puzzled frown. "At least I don't think so. We're not always privy to whatever's standard at State these days."

Mom Shanda shrugged. "Would only help in certain situations, anyway."

"What would it hurt? Unless vampires can't be around salt. That's not something you have to worry about, is it?" Mom swooped to the fridge to refill Carrington's tea.

"Moms, this is a unit of police officers with specific talents," Erasmus said with an exasperated laugh. "It's not *Supernatural*."

They both ignored him, still focused on Carrington. Mom Shanda waved a fork toward him. "You see a lot of ghosts on your cases? Apparitions? Possible demon possessions?"

"No, ma'am. To be honest, a good ninety percent of our calls are nonsense. People who swear they have ghosts, but they only have an old, creaking house. People who see unfamiliar animals and report them as monsters. That sort of thing. I don't recall a single, legitimate ghost call since I've been with the department."

"There." Mom Shanda planted her fist on the table. "The boy doesn't need salt."

"What do you carry, then?" Mom wasn't going to let this go, so Erasmus stopped trying to intervene. "Sage? Garlic? Iron? Whiskey?"

Carrington's ears had that pink hue they picked up when he was embarrassed or uncomfortable. "Most days, I have a radio, a handgun and pepper spray. I also have a partner with a mean right hook." He cleared his throat and started to sink in his seat. "Ras is right. We're just a bunch of unplaceable officers that State Paranormal stuck in one precinct. Except for Lieutenant Dunfee, we don't have much in the way of magical training. While that's probably not a good thing for people like Vikash Soren, who really should have been trained to control the psychic destruction his brain is capable of, we're not a high priority."

"They do have someone starting to teach the officers. Unofficially." Erasmus couldn't let Carrington keep going and getting more morose with each sentence. "She's a little unorthodox, I guess. But she's very powerful."

"Do we know her?" Mom Shanda looked over her forkful of stew at Erasmus.

Erasmus glanced at Carrington, not certain if this was information they could share, but Carrington answered for him, "Pecca Teecosi."

"Teecosi...Teecosi..." Mom mused. "That's a familiar name. Didn't your Auntie Louisa know a Teecosi?"

"She did, but that's a long time ago." Mom Shanda pushed her chair back. "That was way back during the Korean War. I haven't heard of any Teecosis in the city since then. Maybe one of the relatives moved back. Don't know. Have to get back to work." She put her dishes in the sink and came to give both Carrington and Erasmus bone-crushing hugs before she left the room and tromped up the stairs to her office.

Mom hesitated before she got up. "Did you get enough to eat, Ras? I don't want you to rush. You're all bones these days."

"I've always been all bones, Mom," Erasmus said with a soft chuckle. "You just forget every time it's been a few days."

"I'll make you a container to take with you. I know you." She shook her fork at him. "You get frozen garbage and eat junk. Doesn't he, Carr?"

"Sometimes, yes." Carrington laughed at Erasmus' irritated glare. "I refuse to lie to your mother for you. He's not doing too badly these days, ma'am. And we both try to encourage each other to better habits."

"Good." Mom bustled about finding a container and its matching lid. "I like this one, Ras. You'd better keep him."

# Chapter Five

"Visitor for you, Carr," Alex pointed back toward the front of the building as he made his way to his desk after lunch.

Puzzled, Carrington straightened from his customary crumple and spotted Dr. Hayes peering into the squad room. "Dr. Hayes? Is everything all right?"

"Oh, Carrington, there you are." The smile appeared relieved, probably due to being saved from an awkward moment at a police station. "Yes, yes, fine. All's well. I made the mistake of mentioning I would be down this way to your mother and she had the odd idea that I might be able to bully you into an answer where she's failed."

"What answer, sir?"

"You know how your mother is. She's insisting that you and your librarian come to dinner on Thursday." Dr. Hayes cleared his throat uncomfortably. "I know she can be…demanding, but you could return her calls, old sock, old bean."

"I'm so sorry she's involved you in our family power struggles." Carrington rubbed at his forehead. It was far too early for a Mom-induced stress headache. "I'll be sure to call her before we start patrols. I can't apolo —"

Audacity skittered to a stop between them, dancing from one front paw to the other, staring up at Dr. Hayes, and making a one-kitten ruckus of herself.

"What's the meaning of this, Cadet?" Carrington said as he picked her up.

*Miiiiiw, mmrrehh! Miiii-iiiireh!*

"What in the —" Carrington realized she was waving a paw at Dr. Hayes' tiepin. His silver tiepin, in fact, which happened to be in the shape of a skull. The very *same* skull he had recently picked up out of disturbed grave dirt. "Audacity, hush. I see it. This may sound odd, Dr. Hayes, but did you happen to have a set of cufflinks to match that tiepin?"

Dr. Hayes' forehead crinkled and he lifted his tie to glance down at the fastening. "Ah. The little *memento mori*. I did have a set of cufflinks, but I've managed to lose one somewhere along the way. One cufflink does me no good at all, so the poor tiepin is now a solo piece."

"I'm sorry to hear that." Carrington tried for as light a tone as he could. The shock of seeing that particular skull on someone he'd known since he was small had made him lightheaded. "Do you have any idea when the cufflink wandered off?"

"Oh..." Dr. Hayes' mouth turned down in an exaggerated way that indicated he was trying to dredge up some piece of information. "I don't think I've seen it since last Halloween or so."

*Of course. Probably stolen for some specific properties of the metal.* So that meant the necromancer was someone who knew Dr. Hayes, at least socially. "Truly a shame. It's a beautifully detailed piece. I'll keep an eye out just in case. And I promise to call Mother."

"Yes, please." Dr. Hayes' distracted smile returned. "Oh, and one last item. I am sorry. Putting you on the spot like this. I may have suggested that you bring guests of your own. Simply to alleviate your mother's single-minded focus on you, though I would never tell her that. She, ah, asserted that it was a splendid idea."

*Miw?* Audacity put a paw on his cheek.

"I'm all right, little one." Carrington kissed the top of her head. "Though I wish I could still take aspirin. Thank you, Dr. Hayes. Again, I'm sorry you had to go to the trouble."

"No trouble. Not in the slightest." Dr. Hayes lifted his hand in a cheery wave to the squad room before he turned to leave. "Nice to see you all!"

Some waves and murmurs came in return before half the squad collapsed in gales of laughter. Carrington let it go on for a moment while he let Audacity down to run back to her dad. Kash wandered over with his coffee cup, no sign on his face that he'd found the exchange amusing.

"Interesting man, Dr. Hayes."

"He is. A little scattered, not always terribly present in the real world." Carrington offered a one-shoulder shrug. "But he lives in his books." He raised his voice just enough to be heard over the hilarity. "Since it's all so terribly funny, who's coming with me to dinner?"

The silence felt like all sound had been sucked from the world except for Kash sipping his coffee. "I'll go."

Kyle, still red-faced from laughing, gaped at his husband in horror. "Aw, man!"

"You don't have to go," Kash said with the barest hint of a smile.

"But that would look bad. Damn it, Kash."

Amanda was still snickering. "You know I'll go, Carr. At least your family knows me. And I like annoying your mom."

"I'll go," Eva said softly, her eyes flicking to Amanda and back. "If you want."

"If your mom will have me, happy to go as moral support," Jeff offered. "Vance?"

Vance, who, oddly enough, had *not* been laughing, now turned an interesting shade of pink. "I, um, have Pecca. I mean *lessons!* Lessons with Pecca."

"Was I supposed to be there?" Jeff's forehead creased in confusion.

"No, um, she wants me to try with different conduits. So, Jeremy and Greg."

"Oh, good. Thought I forgot something." Jeff turned back to Carrington. "Is that enough?"

"Plenty. Thank you." Carrington strode back to his desk, girding his loins for a mom call. "Oh, and Greg, since you're manning the phones today, let's try to recreate the guest list from the reception here. I want to try to cross-reference people Dr. Hayes might see on a semi-regular basis. Someone with the opportunity to steal his cufflink. Probably someone who lives alone and has money to back up the society connections. Maybe we can narrow down the possible identity of our necromancer."

Carrington even managed to be pleasant with his mom on the phone, though he wanted to say several dozen sarcastic things about bullying friends of the family into doing her dirty work and leaving enough vague non-messages to overload his voicemail. She seemed taken aback by how *many* friends he proposed to bring for dinner, but he had to give her credit, she accepted the other guests without a single unpleasant comment.

"You remember we have Pecca tonight, yeah?" Amanda asked when he'd finished.

"Of course."

"You, me, Alex and Ras."

"Yes, yes." Carrington leaned around his monitor to glare at his partner. "What are you saying? Or not saying?"

"Just wanna be sure you don't 'forget' Ras. 'Cause I know how your brain works."

"I'm hurt and appalled. And you know me too well. But Ras and I had a talk last night. I fully concede that I can't wrap him in packing materials and put him on a shelf." Carrington retreated to his own side of the desk with a leaden-hearted sigh. "He should be able to help protect himself if he can. I simply wish he hadn't registered with Pecca as paranormally gifted."

"Yeah, then you could just tell him it's police business and no place for civilians," Amanda replied in a pointed mutter.

"Don't pick, Amanda. This is hard enough for me."

"He's a grown man. Just reminding you."

"Busybody."

"Control freak."

"It's not as if—" Carrington broke off at a commotion—clanks and thuds, then another set of footsteps coming from the front hall.

Amanda stood to lean over the monitors. "Carr? What?"

"Someone's coming. Several someones." He sprang out of his chair again and hurried to the front of the squad room just as the shadows in the front hall resolved into people. "Oh...crumbs."

"Good morning, Seventy-Seventh!" Captain Valbuena addressed the squad with a charming smile, one ren behind him to take his coat and four more at his back as if they were some sort of Praetorian Guard. "We've arrived to take care of your necromancer issue."

* * * *

It was an afternoon of rapid-fire meetings and swift, clandestine conversations in twos and threes. Lieutenant Dunfee agreed with Carrington that, yes, it would be lovely if the captain could resolve the issue, but they had to continue preparations in case he failed. The sticking point came when the lieutenant insisted that Carrington brief Valbuena.

"We've been targeted all along, ma'am, I'm sure of it," Carrington said through gritted teeth. "If he comes in here and tries to micromanage—"

"It's his right." Lieutenant Dunfee snapped the pencil she held, then put the pieces down carefully. "This is chain of command, Loveless. I can't change it and I won't allow you to circumvent it."

"Ma'am." The word was stiff and bitter. *I thought I'd gotten past most of this.*

"We're in a dangerous situation here with no room for prima donnas." Her voice grew soft and dangerous. "Either you find the professional I know is in there, or you start rethinking your career path."

"Yes, ma'am." Carrington rubbed at both temples with his fingertips. "Profound apologies. He's a seasoned investigator with an experienced team and I'll keep reminding myself of that. Though if State understands we have a serious necromancer issue, I'm not sure why more resources weren't allocated. And what if he finds out about Pecca's involvement?"

"State believes this is the necessary level of response. We work with what they give us, as always." Lieutenant Dunfee stared at her monitor for an uncomfortable moment. "Concerning Pecca, Richard's less constricted by tradition than his peers. If he makes it an issue, I'll speak to him. We need all possible personnel on this one. If I have to deputize her, I will."

"Yes, ma'am." *I can do this. I can.*

She flapped a hand at him. "Out of my office. Go do something constructive."

Carrington, who knew the routine better than any other officer, dutifully fled. As he gathered files and data into a single pile, he debated asking Kash to assist. *No, I can't keep using other people as a buffer. Gods, I feel like I'm six again.*

Finally, he approached where Captain Valbuena was chatting with Alex. "At your convenience, Captain, I'll brief you and your staff in the conference room."

"I'm glad someone is. The file I received was dreadfully disjointed." Valbuena turned his head to speak into the radio at his shoulder. "Mina, stop fussing with equipment checks and bring everyone in for a briefing."

The response was immediate and crisp. "Yes, sir."

Valbuena flashed him a smile. "We'll join you in a moment, Officer."

The sigh managed to stay suppressed until Carrington reached the conference room. He didn't expect warm and fuzzy from another vamp, but by now he thought they'd be beyond the casually dismissive attitude. With Alex, he showed a warmer, more human side and Valbuena interacted well with most of the squad — almost to the point of friendly. He did still demonstrate a virulent dislike of Edgar. Carrington supposed he'd accept almost invisible over open hostility.

Carrington took the head of the table and concentrated on not fidgeting, still as stone as the rens marched in. Most rens were drawn from paranormal SWAT teams — highly disciplined, paramilitary units heavy on combat and weapons training, so gods forbid they would amble or saunter. He understood the need. A normal vampire officer was far too vulnerable during the day and certain paranormal criminals had been known to try to take advantage. Still, it all fed into the superiority complex from which so many vamps suffered.

Two women, three men, all of them taller than Carrington, all fit and toned — they revealed all the pertinent details about the captain's sexuality. While sex wasn't *required* for feeding, the sexual overtones of the act were inescapable and most vampires preferred rens with whom they could form a permanent bond.

Valbuena strode in last, closed the door and threw himself into a chair with casual insouciance. "Ladies, gentleman, this is Officer Loveless, senior staff here. Give him your undivided attention, if you would, please."

In his head, Carrington had them all answering, *yes, your Imperial Highness*, but he put that and the obvious lack of introductions firmly to the side. They were a silent and hyper-focused audience, quivering with barely leashed energy like a pack of mastiffs waiting for the attack command, taking notes in various ways as Valbuena looked on with the air of an indulgent family patriarch.

Carrington reached the end of his briefing with, "That's everything we have right now, sir. Though I should mention Ms. Teecosi is acting as a consultant on this one…"

"And?" Valbuena's half-smile was far too smug.

"I've been asked to inform you that she's engaging in some training of our personnel. Off-duty. Unofficially."

The smug faded into concern. "Hmm. I see. I assume Lieutenant Dunfee is keeping this off record entirely."

"Yes, sir. Her position is that what officers do on their own time, as long as it's legal, is not her business."

Valbuena leaned back in his chair on a long exhale. "I sympathize with Mia's position. If this becomes an issue, we may need to revisit turning a blind eye. I'm well acquainted with Ms. Teecosi's power and proficiency, but she is an unregistered practitioner, largely self-taught." Abruptly, he turned to his staff. "Questions?"

"Sir." Mina, whom Carrington had seen on previous visits, raised her hand. "A full necromancy kit should've been done at the grave sites."

*A what?* Carrington fished desperately in his memory for what that could be.

"I see from Officer Loveless' expression that N-kits are unfamiliar," Valbuena purred. "While we're on loan here, please try to be sensitive to the fact that this precinct doesn't have the up-to-date resources we have at State." Valbuena gestured in Carrington's direction.

"Necromancers leave distinct signatures in their magic, their methods and goals. From magical residue studies and other detritus, we're often able to identify known necromancers in the national database."

Carrington clamped his jaw shut so he wouldn't be caught gaping. *There's a database? Of necromancers? Of course there is.*

One of the larger men, the one with darker skin and the hint of a European accent, raised his hand next. "Sir, it appears that this one's leaving evidence behind, though. He wants someone to know who he is."

Carrington nodded. "Yes, that's wh—"

"Exactly, Kadan. This one is *un égoïste*. He's planning something grand and wants his genius known."

*I suppose I'll be the good provincial peasant and sit quietly.* Carrington kept as neutral a demeanor as possible, shoving his annoyance into a concrete-walled inner box.

The captain dismissed his staff after giving them specific assignments, but he stayed, tapping a finger on the table and staring at Carrington.

"You still don't like me, do you?"

Carrington tried to protest. Nothing came out.

"You see me as arrogant and high-handed. Privileged. Spoiled." Valbuena frowned at the table. "Some see you that way, too, you know."

"Captain…" Carrington managed to unclench his fists. "Whether I *like* you or not is immaterial. Yes, less chilly interactions would make things more comfortable. But I do want you to know that I recognize three things. First, that my issues with other vampires are, mostly, not your fault. That's a personal item. I'm working on it. Second is that your experience far surpasses anything we can offer here, outside of

Lieutenant Dunfee's. Third is that you *do* interact with most of my officers in a respectful manner, and I appreciate that."

The finger tapping returned. "Anything else you feel the need to say to me while we have a moment's privacy?"

Carrington leaned forward, hands clasped on the table. "Just this, sir, and I didn't bring it up in front of your staff because it's just a suspicion, a feeling. I have no direct evidence."

"Yes?"

"I think there's a chance one of our officers, Jeff Gatling, is being directly targeted."

For one horrible moment, Carrington thought his fears would be dismissed as Valbuena stared at him. Then he nodded, his focus on some distant thought. "I'll take it under advisement. Thank you for trusting me with that."

He rose and left without another word, allowing Carrington to have a moment alone with his headache.

Back in the squad room, Greg waved him over. "Went through the guest list, Carr. Narrowed down the possibles to five — men living alone, who own property where they could keep, you know, necromancy stuff, and had recent contact with Dr. Hayes." He pushed a list across the desk. "Your brother's one of them."

Carrington snorted. "My brother's an idiot who can't recall which fork to use for dessert. We can rule him out."

"Yeah, always wondered how that happened," Greg murmured. "Sure he's your brother?"

"Genetics are a wondrous and frightening thing."

Carrington picked up the list to stare at the names as if one would leap out and scream *necromancer*. Andrew

Hartigan, a youngish widower who lived alone in the huge pile of his family's mansion. Edward Ballard, family money from the coal baron days converted to high-powered banking. Jessup Penrose, another academic with old money backing, though Penrose was an art historian rather than a linguist. Last was Lawrence Dorrance, who had inherited his mother's fortune and sold the family business to top off the pile. Theater, art, music, Lawrence stuck his fingers in everything, even a small publishing company, but he had something of a black thumb and his ventures tended to fail.

Of the remaining list, only Ballard seemed unlikely. While he lived alone, social events at his house were far too frequent with far too many people overrunning his property for the privacy a necromancer would need. The rest, he couldn't rule out. He set the list in front of Amanda when he returned to his desk.

She frowned at the names. "Okay. So what now? I mean, no probable cause, not like we can search houses."

"I'll just pop by and ask to see their necromantic room, then, shall I? Yes, that should work." Carrington put his still-aching head on his desk. "I don't know quite yet. Perhaps the Royal Vampire Guard will have it resolved by dinnertime and we can all sleep soundly tonight."

"Gonna start calling them the RVG. Sounds better than *the rens*." Amanda leaned around the desk. "Not a great meeting?"

"Could have been so much worse. I still feel like I shrank several inches every time one of them spoke."

"Maybe we should ask Pecca about vampire stuff for headaches. You've been getting a lot of them."

"I don't have the foggiest notion why *that* would be."

Amanda snorted as she stood up from her desk and stretched. "You ready? I can stick you in the trunk and we can pretend you're a royal vamp."

"Thank you, but no. Having a tire jack digging into my ribcage is not my idea of a good time."

Patrols were quiet that day, which seemed almost obscene. Animated corpses lurked somewhere in the city. All the citizens focused on their daily routines shouldn't have been strolling happily in the sunshine. There should have been ominous yellow clouds. Thunder. Screaming and mayhem. Random lightning strikes, at the very least.

Perhaps it was a little sad that the highlight of his afternoon was returning to the condo with Amanda to change and pick up Ras. As soon as he'd exchanged his uniform for jeans and a T-shirt, Carrington flopped onto the sofa where Ras was reading, buried his head against his librarian's stomach and breathed deeply of his scent.

"Hey. I'm still here. Just saying," Amanda called over from the kitchen area.

Erasmus' chuckle vibrated through Carrington's skull, which felt oddly wonderful. Better still when Erasmus stroked his hair. "What are you doing?"

"Aromatherapy. Working wonders for my headache." Carrington rolled onto his back. "Did you have dinner?"

"Mmm. Had a sandwich." Erasmus placed his bookmark and set his reading aside. "I guess I'm too nervous to eat much. *You* should eat before we go."

Amanda set a blood pack and Carrington's thermos on the coffee table. "He can eat in the car. I'll drive."

"Five more minutes, Manda. Please." Carrington attempted his best tragic puppy eyes.

"This right here," she said to Erasmus. "This is what I deal with all day."

Erasmus, the traitor, responded by laughing and sliding out from under Carrington. "Come on, Mr. Fishing For Sympathy. People are waiting for us."

Carrington grumbled but allowed Erasmus to pull him up and out the door. Not letting go of his hand until they reached the car almost made up for the terribly cruel treatment.

"A cop goes to this invisible house with a vampire and a librarian," Amanda muttered as she started the engine. "Sounds like the start of a really bad joke."

"And it may well still be." Carrington raised his thermos in salute. "The night is young."

* * * *

Erasmus hesitated with his hand on the door when they reached Pecca's. "That car isn't Alex's."

An older Mustang sat opposite Pecca's obscured house. Not a big car aficionado, Erasmus couldn't have pinpointed the year, but the pristine condition and its paint job of deep, shiny red impressed him.

"That's Virago's baby." Amanda nodded to it. "I helped him put a refurbished engine in that thing. Block was cracked when he bought it."

"I don't recall Vance being on today's list." Carrington eased out of the car with languid grace and drew off his shades since the sun had set some time ago. "Is he not doing well with lessons?"

Amanda gave him an odd look. "Yeah, okay. Let's go with that."

"What? What have I missed now?" Carrington snapped, then realization crept over his annoyed expression. "Ah. Right."

Erasmus poked him in the ribs. "Okay, so what am *I* missing?"

"I think our Officer Virago may have a crush on Ms. Teecosi."

Carrington spun to address the spot where the house should be when a growling engine rumble turned down the street. A sleek black motorcycle sped toward them, driven by a tall man in a mirror-visored helmet and a black leather jacket.

"Could be trouble." Amanda reached into the car for her jacket. "Ras, keep the car between him and you."

The motorcyclist pulled up short of Amanda's car, revved the engine twice before shutting it down then pulled off his helmet to a muted groan from Carrington. Blond hair spilled out unbound and the man on the bike shot them a bright, fanged grin.

The tic in Carrington's jaw was visible from twenty paces. "Captain, I didn't realize Pecca had included you in these sessions."

"Oh, she hasn't. Not yet." Captain Valbuena locked his helmet in the compartment behind the seat. "But I'm too curious to stay away."

Carrington was having none of it. "You're here to check up on us. To make certain her teaching doesn't stray too far from what State allows."

Just as Erasmus feared the small standoff would become ugly for someone, Alex's blue Wrangler turned onto Pecca's street, distracting both vampires nicely. Alex Wolf was no fool, though, and he probably picked up more undercurrent by scent than Erasmus could from observation. His eyes were wary slits as he parked and climbed out of his car, and was quick to cross the street and put himself between vampires.

"Sir? Didn't expect you here."

"Good evening, Alex." Valbuena's predatory smile warmed. "It sounded too intriguing to miss."

Alex gave the captain a quick glance up and down. "Where'd the bike come from, sir?"

"Kadan drove it down for me and parked it in the hotel garage. Gives me a little more freedom after sunset."

"Um, did you let Ms. Pecca know you were coming? We don't want you getting tossed a hundred yards again."

Carrington's expression brightened. "She did that?"

"Yeah," Alex growled and shook his head. "Please let me go first, sir. And if she doesn't want you here…"

Valbuena held up a hand in surrender. "I'll go. I promise."

"Okay." Alex took a quick glance up and down the street. "Rens?"

"They know I don't need them at night." Valbuena's tone was light, but a tiny hint of guilt might have lurked underneath.

Alex turned a direct and disturbed glare at him. "They don't know you're here, do they, sir?"

"They're a text message away. Is the inquisition complete now?"

With a sigh that didn't quite include an eye roll, Alex stomped to the other side of the street and called to the empty air, "Ms. Pecca? It's Officer Wolf."

A vertical line of light opened against the dusk, Alex leaning toward it to speak in soft, urgent tones. Erasmus couldn't hear a thing, but both vampires obviously could since Carrington got that smug *I'm not smiling* look and Captain Valbuena's ears gained a distinct pink tinge. Finally, Alex waved them to come ahead and vanished behind the invisible door.

The little blue and yellow patchwork dog ran out to greet them, barking and dancing around their legs. Erasmus scooped him up so no one would step on him and was rewarded with licks from a corduroy tongue.

"Awfully cute." Carrington reached over to pet the cloth head. "One of Pecca's safe creations, I take it?"

"He is. I only saw a few of her created friends, but Alex says she has quite a menagerie."

"What's his name?"

"Patches."

Carrington extended a foot to feel for the step Alex had ascended. "Of course it is."

Pecca waited in the front hall for them with what appeared to be a ferret made of felt scraps in her arms. "Officer Wolf went back to the kitchen with Officer Firestarter. We'll work in there. Officer Amanda, nice to see you again. Mr. Librarian, Officer Vampire." She extended a hand to Carrington, whispering soft words as she pulled him through the doorway. "Excuse me. I need a word with Captain Vampire who needs to be more polite than this."

When Carrington looked like he wanted to stay to eavesdrop, Amanda herded them to the kitchen. The only words Erasmus could pick out were *observe* and *unofficial* from the captain and *invited first* from Pecca.

"Well," Pecca began as she entered the kitchen with a definite flounce. "Captain Vampire will be with us for class. As long as he behaves."

"Love the ferret," Amanda offered as a quick change in topic. "Is its name Scraps?"

"No, no." Pecca's airy, musical laugh seemed to bring the lights up in the kitchen a few notches. "That's a silly name for a ferret. This is Theodora."

She placed the ferret on the floor where it galumphed up to Captain Valbuena, chittered at him irritably, then galloped off. As interesting as the vampire drama was, Erasmus was drawn to the sight of Vance sitting at the kitchen table, frowning in concentration as he cut shapes out of folded up pieces of paper—paper snowflakes, to be exact.

"Officer Firestarter has been helping me prepare." Pecca put a hand on Vance's shoulder and he stilled, as if afraid of startling her if he moved. "We have three sources and a conduit." She pulled Vance's chair back and urged him away from the table, gently disengaging the scissors from his fingers when it looked like he'd forgotten he was holding them. "And what I'd like to show you is that conduits can work small magics even without makers if there's enough power available."

"Unlike the officers here, I've never had even a tiny psychic ability show up, Ms. Pecca." Erasmus glanced down at his hands. "Doubtful that I'll manage anything."

"Not everyone has a talent leak through, like seeing things that were or moving pencils." Pecca glided over to take his hand and lead him to the table. "You are a clear conduit. I feel the world rushing through you. Once, every child would've known. We had covens and knew workings were stronger together."

"But this is all so old-fashioned, Ms. Pecca," the captain said softly, though Erasmus could have slapped him for the condescension in his tone. "No one learns that way anymore."

Pecca had crossed the room before Erasmus knew she'd moved, standing nose to nose with Captain Valbuena. "And that, Captain Vampire, is why my witch wind can toss you out of my house and all you can say is *oof*."

"He didn't even have a chance for that," Alex grumbled. "Please don't. I had to carry him back last time."

Pecca shoved a curl out of her eyes. "I know you mean well, Captain. But this evening it's learn or leave. No peanut gallery."

"Ma'am." Captain Valbuena retreated to a kitchen stool in the corner, clearly perturbed but silent when Flap landed on his head.

"Pecca." Carrington held out a hand as she came back across the room. "This won't hurt him in any way, will it?"

"You are such a sweetie." Pecca leaned in for a peck on Carrington's cheek. "I won't hurt your gorgeous lover. It's hard to hurt someone acting as a conduit. But you *can* hurt a source. Take too much, too fast and — "

"Oof," Amanda supplied.

Pecca beamed at her as she took Erasmus' hand again. "Exactly. So. Mr. Librarian, I'll feed power through you first. That way you can feel."

"What are we going to do?" Erasmus tried for brave, but his voice still cracked.

"We're going to make snowflakes dance."

Pecca stretched a hand out toward the table, her long fingers describing waves in the air. At first, Erasmus watched in fascination, though he didn't expect any change in himself. When it began, it was a slow trickle, a low-level electrical tingle at his core. The trickle became a tug, then a surge. Erasmus gasped as the surge became a flood of sensation, hot and cool at once, sharp and painful in the way a half-remembered shining moment is, not flowing *from* him but *through* him, rushing in from the magic house, the people in the room, the grass and wildflowers outside, the wind, the earth…

*Too much, it's too much. I'm going to fall or fly off.* Just as he thought it, though, the feeling of being swept away subsided. The rushing remained but Pecca's arm around his waist steadied him. She flicked a gesture toward the table and Erasmus *felt* the magic turn in her grasp, felt it reach for the paper scattered there. One by one, the snowflakes rose and unfolded to spin and dance, bumping each other, righting and swooping off to spin again.

He leaned into Pecca, overcome by the simple wonder of it all. Maybe it was strange to think it just then, but Vance's snowflake artistry astounded him. They were delicate and intricate — so beautiful.

"Good. You're doing so well," Pecca murmured close to his ear. Her face was young, but in that moment, she felt ancient to him, the priestess of an elder power. "Now give me less. Think about shutting a valve slowly. Or making the pipe narrower."

"I don't know how," he whispered, aware on some level of clinging to her arm.

"You feel it. The stream running through you. Surround it. Focus on it. Tighten, tighten, tighten."

All of Erasmus' muscles strained with the effort, though the actual doing was in his mind. He thought of the magic coursing through a stone tunnel, racing through the dark toward daylight, and he thought the stones smaller, smaller, smaller…

The snowflakes abruptly dropped to the table.

"Did you…? Did he…?" Carrington slid a careful arm around Erasmus as Pecca released him. "Holy mother of storms."

"That could all have been—" Captain Valbuena's sentence cut off with an upheld hand as an apology.

"I'll get to you, Captain Vampire. You can be useful today, too." Pecca turned to Carrington. "But not yet."

Carrington's arm tightened around Erasmus, probably in a reflex protective moment. "You've said I'm a source, Ms. Pecca. It sounds as if I don't do anything besides acting as a magical battery."

"Oh, I like that." Pecca's smile for him was all sun-kissed warmth. "It's true. A conduit gathers and passes magic on. Sometimes, like with Officer Kyle, a conduit also magnifies. A source only gives."

"Again, and I'm terribly sorry if I'm being dense, but I don't understand what I would need to learn."

Pecca stroked his arm gently. "To give."

That poleaxed Carrington. Erasmus knew him well enough by now to pick up the hint of panic in his eyes — not fear-of-the-unknown panic but what-if-I-fail panic.

"Hey." Erasmus gave him a hard squeeze. "I think you're perfect. Doesn't mean you have to be perfect *all* the time."

Carrington leaned into him with half a smile. *Better.*

"Someone powerful enough can *take* from you."

Pecca stretched a hand out toward Captain Valbuena's corner in what seemed a casual gesture. Erasmus thought she meant someone powerful like him until the captain gasped and slid from his stool to his knees. Behind Pecca, the snowflakes danced madly, lit with an eerie blue glow. She dropped her hand. The snowflakes tumbled. Captain Valbuena slapped a hand down on the kitchen tiles to steady himself.

"What in all hells was *that*?" he snarled, gentility buried under fury.

"That was taking, Captain Vampire. Now they see how easy it is to take from someone unprotected. Even someone powerful."

"I am *not* an object lesson, Ms. Teecosi!"

Alex let out a distressed huff as he made his way over and held out a hand. "Hate to say it, but you were a pretty good one, sir. Are you hurt?"

"No," Valbuena snapped, but he accepted the hand and amended his tone. "No. Thank you, Alex. Only my pride. It was shocking rather than painful."

Pecca filled the kettle and put it on the stove. Apparently, there would be tea, maybe as a sort of apology since even normal vampires could drink certain herbal teas. "Mama always said never to let vampires in the house and here I've let in two. Everything's all higgledy-piggledy and time feels like it's squashing itself. You're almost strong enough to take this sorcerer by yourself, Captain. If you'd been taught. But I don't think I have time. I can show all of you what you are. I can even teach you a little about working together. We have to hope it makes all of us strong enough."

"Probably not the most traditional coven, are we?" Erasmus' stomach was doing macramé. Yes, he knew things were bad, scary bad, but Pecca's worries hit harder than an actor zorpse attack.

"Weirdest coven in history." Pecca shoved her curls back from her face and reached for tea canisters. "Ginger tea for Officer Vampire. For vampire headaches. Up on the top shelf by you, Vance."

It could have been a slip, the unembellished first name when Pecca didn't use them for anyone else, but

Erasmus didn't think so. Vance's eyes widened as he hurried to get the ginger tea down for her.

Vance clutched the tea box to his chest. "You don't read minds...do you?"

"That's very rare. It's also rude to do on purpose." Pecca halted in her fluttering with mugs. "I don't. But you don't need to snoop around in people's heads to feel pain."

The rest of the evening passed without further confrontation as Captain Valbuena took on the role of student. Erasmus learned to draw power, which wasn't as hard as he thought now that he knew what to *feel* for, and he practiced with everyone in the room. It was easiest—the flow was best, at least—with Carrington. With him, it was as if the magic picked up particles from Carrington, and Erasmus felt the love pouring out with the stream. He couldn't help a smile at the confirmation of something he'd suspected, but that Carrington hadn't been able to say yet. Erasmus would never rush him. He'd say the words when he felt comfortable enough.

"Why does that happen?" Erasmus asked after he'd played conduit for Vance with Alex as the source, which was a lot like pulling wisdom teeth. "That it works better with Carr? Is he a bigger reservoir?"

Pecca hopped up on the counter, swinging her feet. "Sources have different ways of accessing power. Officer Amanda pulls little snips from her surroundings all the time and doesn't know it. Officer Wolf is a broad source, like a marsh. Officer Vampire is a deep well, but he's connected to you already. He surrenders to you."

The sexual connotations were too obvious and Erasmus' face burned. "I see."

She took pity on him after that and left him alone while she worked with the captain and Vance, taking them through an exercise in control where Valbuena made the snowflakes dance and Vance sent tiny flames waltzing between them. He only singed a couple of paper edges and the concentrated practice took the edge off *him* enough that he laughed when Pecca made an intricate snowflake from his airborne flames.

"It's getting late." She caught Vance's hand to stop him. "And I need to redo spells to secure the house. Goodnight, everyone. Pray to whatever gods listen to you that the sorcerer isn't ready yet."

"That's not ominous at all," Carrington muttered as he placed his tea mug in the sink, but he turned to Pecca before they left. "Thank you. For teaching us and for the tea. I do feel better."

"Good," she called after them as they made their way to the front door. "Sex helps, too."

Poor Carrington. The tops of his ears were as pink as the roses in Pecca's wallpaper before they'd closed the door behind them.

# Chapter Six

Carrington was silent on the way back to his condo, though it didn't appear to Erasmus to be a distressed silence. More of a processing one. They said goodnight to Amanda at the curb and climbed the stairs hand-in-hand. Carrington finally spoke as he unlocked the door.

"Well, that was…"

"Interesting? Enlightening? Scary?" Erasmus supplied.

"Yes to all of those." Carrington slipped his shoes off in the foyer then wandered into the living room. "Also incredibly strange. I've been *aware* of magic before, but I've never been aware of it *inside* me."

Erasmus snickered at the innuendo, which turned into a laugh at Carrington's glare. "I know what you mean. It's not like I never had contact with magic before. There are pagans of all sorts in my family and actual practitioners like Auntie Mia. But I never thought I had any real connection to it."

"I'm with you there. My family's idea of magic concerns stage magicians, who are occasionally amusing, but frowned upon." Carrington stopped his meandering to face Erasmus, heat sparking in his eyes. "I won't deny it was exciting, though. In ways completely inappropriate in front of one's colleagues."

Erasmus stalked toward him. "Was it? It was the part about surrendering, wasn't it?"

"Certainly didn't help matters. That and the comment about sex helping a headache."

"You *have* been getting a lot of them lately." Erasmus reached him and ran his fingertips along Carrington's hairline. "Do you still have one?"

"N—" Carrington stopped his automatic denial on a hard swallow, his voice dropping to a husky whisper. "Maybe a little."

"We can't have that, can we?" Erasmus tugged Carrington's T-shirt out of his jeans so he could slide his hands up that cool, hard-muscled back.

"It does tend to curtail meaningful conversation."

Erasmus slid his hands under the waistband of Carrington's jeans, an admittedly tight fit, and teased along the top curve of his ass. "Maybe surrendering will clear that up, too."

A strangled moan vibrated in Carrington's chest and Erasmus couldn't help a grin. He tugged Carrington's T-shirt over his head and tossed it on a nearby chair. When Carrington tried to reciprocate, Erasmus swatted his hands away. "No, no. That's not surrendering. Hands to yourself."

A hint of a smile tugged at Carrington's lips as he laced his hands behind his head, showing off his upper body assets to their fullest. Erasmus leaned in to place a soft kiss on his lips, then one on each biceps as he undid the fly of Carrington's jeans.

"I could leave you like this for a bit," Erasmus whispered against his throat. "Maybe go grab a snack."

"Please don't." Carrington's answer was breathy, ragged. "I'll beg if I must."

That single word—*please*—send a spike of want through Erasmus. "Don't think that should be necessary quite yet."

Instead of teasing him further, Erasmus pushed the jeans down over Carrington's hips and let them fall under the weight of wallet and keys to the floor. Carrington let out a huff, not quite an exclamation, as his erection sprang free of the denim, his eyes squeezed shut as Erasmus helped him get his feet free as well.

With little prods and tugs, Erasmus got him to the sofa. "You can have your hands to lie down. Then put them right back."

It was a dizzying sensation, having this powerful man acquiesce without question, and more than dizzying when Carrington had stretched out in all his frost-pale glory with his hands tucked behind his head again.

He could have tried something elaborate. Someday he would, with a little planning. Right then, he wanted a taste and wanted to make his vampire moan. Erasmus whipped off his own T-shirt and crawled onto the sofa between Carrington's feet, stroking the insides of his thighs. Completely obliging that evening, Carrington spread his legs wider with a soft sigh.

"Ras—"

"Shh. I've got you. Just relax."

Amazingly, the tension drained from Carrington's arms with those simple words. Erasmus breathed over his cock, smiling when it jumped, then leaned in to suck on Carrington's balls. They weren't cold, not the way his fingers and toes grew cold, but pleasantly cool.

Carrington arched his back and hissed, moaning when Erasmus licked at the skin behind his sac. There, that sound. He wanted more of that. Slowly, letting his lover squirm, Erasmus licked up his shaft. Carrington was so keyed up by the time Erasmus wrapped his lips around him, that he bucked and cried out. Erasmus put a hand on his stomach, stroking in little circles, pressing down until Carrington flopped back again, breathing hard.

Humming in order to drive Carrington even wilder, Erasmus lowered his head until he had nearly all of that gorgeous cock in his mouth.

"Oh gods," Carrington whispered, head flung back on the cushions.

Erasmus took the cue and began a slow progress up and down, with heavy suction one moment, the lightest touch the next. He'd anticipated a few minutes and paced himself, but Carrington's body had other ideas. Within a few strokes, before Erasmus even had time to cup his balls, Carrington cried out, writhing and bucking as he came.

The rush of salt and sweet made Erasmus moan as well, heat rushing through him as he swallowed every drop Carrington offered. He slowed his strokes, letting them both ease down, licking along over-sensitized skin for a few extra squirms.

"Ras?" Carrington's tone wasn't the sleepy, satiated one he'd been anticipating. It was strained... Concerned.

When he opened his eyes, a disorienting sensation shuddered through him. Something wasn't right. This wasn't where they'd started. He lifted his head to find that they'd levitated off the sofa a good ten inches.

"Well, crap."

As soon as he said it, whatever strange magical field they'd created collapsed. They returned to regularly scheduled gravity with a heavy thump.

Carrington clutched at the cushions, still breathing hard. "That was unsettling. Do you suppose that will happen every time now?"

"Something we need to be aware of, that's all," Erasmus stroked his shoulder. "I'm sure we can learn to control it, and if not, we'll have to take certain steps to make sure you stay put."

Carrington chuckled. "I think I like the sound of certain steps. But maybe not all the time. Control. Right. Not that this is the sort of thing I want to bring up in Pecca's classes."

"Ha! No." Erasmus nudged Carrington's hip so he could nestle in beside him. "We'll get it. Practice, practice, practice."

\* \* \* \*

"I don't want to go." Yes, he sounded like a three year old, but Carrington was beyond caring.

Erasmus straightened his shirt collar. "You can't expect your friends to face your mother alone. That wouldn't be fair."

"They wouldn't be alone. Dad will be there."

"Please. He's no help."

"And Dr. Hayes."

Erasmus hooked him by the belt loops and pulled him close, causing parts of Carrington to react in ways completely inappropriate for dinner with one's mother.

"Dr. Hayes is a nice man. But he's not much of a buffer against your mom."

"I suppose." Carrington heaved an exaggerated sigh. "I guess we'll have to throw ourselves on the sacrificial altar."

"As long as there's something wonderful for dessert, I'm good with that." Erasmus gave him a swift kiss and smacked Carrington's car keys into his palm. "Let's go, vamp boy. Don't want to start the evening out by giving her an excuse to pick on you when you're late."

Carrington pulled him back in for one more fortifying kiss and murmured against those soft lips, "Tallyho."

The drive over actually buoyed Carrington's spirits. Ras was in a cheerier mood than he had been since the first zorpse attack, and they chatted about normal things — movies they wanted to see, what they should do for Thanksgiving, and the new Beatrix Potter letters the library had received. Everything felt *better* than it had for some time.

Carrington put it down to the investigation closing in on the necromancer and the realization that they might have the resources to meet the threat if it came to a magical confrontation.

His good mood died in the foyer of his parents' house when the housekeeper, Emilia, came to take their jackets.

"She's in a state," Emilia whispered to him. "I could've cooked but she said it was too many people. Then the caterers were late. Your father's in the library. I'd stay out of the kitchen for now."

"Thank you. You may have saved our lives." Carrington planted the expected kiss on her wrinkled cheek.

Human ears most likely couldn't pick it up, but to Carrington, the strident voices from the kitchen were all too clear. He winced at a sharp sentence from his mother and hurried Erasmus in the other direction toward the east wing of the house.

"Vamp senses tingling?" Erasmus asked with a half-aborted ear tug.

"If they got any tinglier, I'd be worried about electrocution." Carrington dredged up a smile as he turned the corner into the library where, thank all the gods, Kash and Kyle were already there talking to Dad.

*About football. Ugh.*

Happily, Kash was one of those people who could converse on any topic, even ones he knew nothing about. He relied on the simple method of asking leading, open-ended questions and let the people around him answer for as long as they pleased. Kyle watched some football here and there, so the conversation they walked into was lively rather than stilted.

"There's Junior!" Dad boomed with forced jocularity. "And Mr. Graham. Nice to see you again."

Carrington took his father's offered hand since hugs would be unmanly, and fought the instinct to roll his eyes so hard they hurt. Dad couldn't think of Ras as his son's *boyfriend*, nor could he react naturally to him because he didn't have the right background, so he opted for super formal and still couldn't get past last names.

If it hurt Erasmus, he never let it show. "Mr. Loveless. Good to see you."

They did the round of handshakes, then went through them again when Jeff arrived on their heels, and Dad went into host mode.

"Junior, do you want one of these?" He hefted his martini.

"Dad, you know I can't."

"Oh, yes. Of course." Dad nudged Jeff with an elbow. "Worse than having an alcoholic uncle."

"I'll join Carr in a water if that's all right," Jeff offered with a tight smile.

Ras gave Jeff a surreptitious pat on the way toward Dad's bar set. "I'd love one, Mr. Loveless, since Carr drove."

That mollified Dad and the atmosphere of the house improved even more due to an apparent cease-fire in the kitchen. Amanda, Eva and Dr. Hayes arrived in a bunch and the rounds of greetings had to start again, with Dad uncertain what to make of Eva. His solution was to ignore her.

"That's a smart tie, Amanda. New?" Dad asked as he mixed a gin and tonic for Dr. Hayes.

Amanda glanced reflexively at her tie, navy with a gold Wonder Woman logo pattern, one of the more understated ones she'd worn to House Loveless. "Yeah, thanks. Last week."

"It fits," Eva said with a shy smile. She'd opted for a simple A-line skirt and button-down, but appeared to be eyeing Amanda's tie with covetous interest. Or maybe it was Amanda. Carrington hadn't quite puzzled out that dynamic yet.

A few minutes later, Mom bustled in to make the rounds, showing no signs at all that she'd just been haranguing her caterer. Perfectly coiffed and dressed casual chic, she sported a necklace Carrington didn't recall seeing before — a gold and diamond pumpkin on a fine rope chain.

"That's pretty, Mom," Carrington nodded to the new shiny as he leaned in to kiss his mom's cheek.

"Very seasonal, isn't it?" She beamed at him and indicated Dr. Hayes across the room. "Garrett brought it for me, with a matching tiepin for your father."

"Handsome present," he agreed and let her continue with her greetings. This *was* a good idea, having multiple guests to distract her. Dr. Hayes had provided more presents than he knew.

Dinner turned out to be a predictably stuffy affair with far too many courses no one was expected to finish and servers whisking the dizzying array of dishes in and out. Kyle appeared personally affronted more than once as wait staff zipped a dish out from under him while he was still engaged in gustatory battle with it. Luckily, a few careful nudges from Kash kept the peace and everyone had the hang of things by the fish course, and an appropriate selection of wines helped relax everyone, of course. Mom even had a small cavalcade of sparkling waters in various flavors for Carrington so he could feel like a partial participant in dinner rather than an outside observer.

Though he did feel like his bladder might burst by the time the dessert and coffee course came around.

Conversation stayed light and not heavily orchestrated as some of Mom's dinners were, and Carrington found he was happier listening to Erasmus in animated conversation with Kash and Dr. Hayes about misconceptions concerning Victorian literature, or Amanda reminiscing with Jeff about parts of the city that were gone or much changed. The whole dinner was actually — nice. Hard to credit, but it was.

They all rose with the hostess when Mom decided dinner was over. "Let's go out to the terrace for a little *digestif.* It's a lovely night, and Mr. Loveless does like his after-dinner cigar."

It had been years since Carrington had seen his father *light* an after-dinner cigar, but he did like having a box to offer around for guests. *Civilized, you see.* Everyone trooped out to the terrace, equipped with cheery brazier heaters and blankets, coffee service, carts for liqueurs, fortified wines and brandies, and plates of chocolates for anyone who could still think about food.

Out here in a less formal setting, Emilia brought Carrington his dinner in a tumbler of black crystal, which he could sip in the shadows without offending his family's sensibilities.

Erasmus took the seat beside him on the divan, with a tiny glass of port. "I thought that went well."

"Surprisingly well." Carrington laced their fingers together. "Mom's attention was divided nicely, which can't have hurt."

"Eh, your mom's not that bad." Amanda flopped into a nearby chair. "She just gets under your skin 'cause she's your mom. I mean, yeah, she's snooty and prejudiced and all. Maybe could be better about one of her sons leading his own life. But she's been trying, Carr."

"Who are you and what have you done with my partner?"

"Ha. You know I'm right."

Carrington sipped. "You generally are. It's hard to let go of years of resentment. You'll have to give me time. But she has been trying. I do see it."

"She does love you, Carrington." Dr. Hayes eased into the other chair in the seating group. "It's difficult to adjust an old worldview that's supported by money and tradition unless there are drastic changes. Drastic, drastic changes."

They sat in the semi-dark in companionable silence, sipping and watching the little fire crackle and pop between them.

Dr. Hayes stirred himself. "I really like your colleagues."

Startled out of his thoughts, Carrington offered a fond smile. "I'm glad to hear that. They're wonderful people."

"So knowledgeable and interesting. And all so talented, too."

A rustling along the arbor vitae snagged Carrington's attention. Something in the rhythm of it didn't sound like night birds or rabbits. He sat up slowly, trying to pinpoint why his alarms were sounding.

"Very much enjoyed talking with them."

The hairs on the backs of Carrington's arms were prickling. Something... He was missing something.

"Which makes what's about to happen such a shame. Such a terrible shame."

Carrington's attention flew back to Dr. Hayes just as the linguist snapped his fingers. Both Carrington's mother and father collapsed to the flagstones and he leaped to his feet. *No. It can't be. No, no, no!* "Mom? Dad?"

Dr. Hayes stood as if he had all the time in the world. "I've always liked you too, my boy. Pity that you're just not as good at puzzles as you used to be. I did try to make it fair."

The air around Dr. Hayes shimmered and dimmed. Empty air replaced where he'd stood, and as if his vanishing had been the signal, dark figures crashed through the shrubbery into the garden.

Kyle, closest to the edge of the terrace, whipped around to face them. "Carr! Zorpses!"

"I see them! Defensive perimeter around the civilians! Ras, stay with my parents!" Carrington stayed long enough for a quick squeeze to his librarian's shoulder before he vaulted the chairs and raced out to meet the incoming horde.

*Damn it, we're short on firepower.* Vance should have been there, and Shira. Carrington dropped to a crouch, trying to count the dead bearing down on them as their gurgling voices assaulted the peace of his mother's garden.

"The street is lined with cars. There's not a breath of fresh air in the neighborhood. The grass don't grow anymore, you can't raise a carrot in the backyard. They should've had a law against apartment houses."

"They told me to take a street-car named Desire, and then transfer to one called Cemeteries and ride six blocks and get off at — Elysian Fields!"

"Martha is a hundred and twenty-five...years old. She weighs somewhat more than that. How old is your wife?"

"Hand in hand from the top of the Eiffel Tower, among the first. We were respectable in those days. Now it's too late. They wouldn't even let us up."

Amid the cacophony of badly enunciated lines, Carrington counted eight — a small horde as hordes went but still daunting. The first to shamble close to him still had most of a jacket. Carrington seized that and hurled the zorpse back into the bushes.

"It's no good, you know," Dr. Hayes said from his right. "They'll just keep coming. And if you break them, I can make more, you see."

"Gods, Dr. Hayes, why?" Carrington shouted though he stayed focused on the shambling deceased actors. "Why are you *doing* this?"

Kyle was on his right now, Kash beside him, and Carrington realized they were making a source-conduit-maker chain while Eva, Jeff and Amanda stayed back as the next line of defense.

"The world is a terrible place, old bean." Instead of sounding triumphant, as evil masterminds were supposed to do, Dr. Hayes sounded tired. "Humans have made a dreadful mess and despite what some of them say, none of them are going to clean it up in time. I knew years ago that saving this world called for new thinking, for a complete change."

"Stella! Stella!"

"I've been out to the greenhouse to pick these. I felt our tomb needed a little brightening. Each time I come back after being away it appears more like a sepulcher!"

"Keep him talking," Kash murmured beneath the disjointed lines from various plays. "And help me pull power."

Carrington tossed another zorpse back into the plantings. "What change? A world of dead actors? Dear gods, why actors?"

Kyle walloped a zorpse in the head with a croquet mallet, one of Dad's good, heavy ones. The zorpse staggered back several steps and fell with a huge dent in its skull, but it immediately began to struggle to its feet again.

"Actors?" Dr. Hayes' weary sigh was somehow audible over the zorpse cacophony. "They're the only ones who've ever answered the summons. From what I've gathered, they think it's a casting call and what actor can resist? So they come, with dreams clinging to them of remembered glory."

"Tomorrow, and tomorrow, and tomorrow, creeps in this petty pace from day to day, to the last syllable of recorded time."

"Honey, you never say nothing new. I listen to you every day, every night and every morning, and you never say nothing new. So you would rather *be* Mr. Arnold than be his chauffeur."

Carrington set his jaw against the pull at the center of his being, trying to relax, to let Kash take what he needed, but it was damn hard. "But what is all of this in aid of? What are the corpses for?"

"My own final act, Carrington." Dr. Hayes' voice came from the other side of the garden now. "I began years ago in an effort to set your precinct up to fail when I learned the city would have a paranormal squad. I couldn't have law enforcement interfering. Subtle manipulation of funding bills. A word in the right ear here and there. Not my intention to involve you directly, but when I saw what you had become, I thought it could only be for the best. A failed vampire to head a pack of failures."

"That explains why things often felt too convenient over the years, but not the purpose." Carrington reached out for Kyle to steady him as Kash pulled power *hard*.

"Despite all odds, and to my enormous irritation, you began to succeed. Destroyed creations of mine. Sidestepped wonderful monsters designed to obliterate the *success* you were not supposed to have." Dr. Hayes gave a rueful laugh. "Again and again, I couldn't clear you out of the way. But now I have the means and the method. I no longer need to. The Piscatory Lords will be summoned. The world will be remade."

"I don't understand. Remade into what?"

Carrington gasped as Kash pressed a palm toward the ground and hurled the power he'd gathered. The earth shuddered and jumped. Four of the zorpses flew apart, limbs and heads sailing through the garden. The remaining four shambled past, not attacking them, but heading straight for Jeff as Carrington feared they would.

With a growl rumbling in his chest, Carrington charged the nearest one. Just as he'd done before, he tackled it, trying to ignore the squelch and stench of rot and slime, and ripped its head from its spine. He wouldn't reach the others in time, but Amanda had just finished handing out croquet mallets as he struggled up from the tangle of zorpse limbs. Holding it like a baseball bat, she swung and took the nearest zorpse's head clean off.

The rest *still* went for Jeff.

"Damn it, Dr. Hayes! Why Jeff?"

"Oh. I thought that was obvious," Dr. Hayes said from the farthest point of the garden. "He's a virgin."

Eva hooked one by the ankle and sent it sprawling, then put a foot on its chest and used the mallet in a golf swing to separate head and body.

"Thanks, Dr. Hayes," Jeff called out. "That wasn't something I needed to be shared."

Jeff took out the last zorpse standing with a vicious wallop and a follow through with one of the wrought iron patio chairs. Carrington had to look away from the mess of smashed bone and goo.

The combatants stood ready for several moments in case they'd missed one, but the garden was quiet and, not surprisingly, Dr. Hayes was gone. Carrington relaxed enough to take stock. His squad appeared unharmed. Erasmus was with his parents, who were waking up. For his part, Carrington was shaky and a little bruised, nothing more serious.

"You were awesome." Eva gazed up at Amanda, hero-worship shining in her eyes.

Amanda chuckled, mallet held on one shoulder like Heracles with his club. "Thanks, kiddo. Not too shabby yourself, there."

"Are they all right?" Carrington hurried over to his mom and dad.

"I think so." Erasmus pointed to the pumpkin necklace and tiepin that were now lying on the stones. "It hit me that Dr. Hayes gave those to them. So I took them off, and your mom and dad started waking up. I guess he didn't want them to see what was happening? I don't know."

Carrington grasped his hands. "Are *you* all right?"

"I'm okay. I think. Yeah." Erasmus leaned his head on Carrington's shoulder. "That was awful. But I'm not hurt or anything."

"I'm glad you're not." Carrington huffed a hard breath and pulled him into a fierce hug. "Though that was only half the question."

"Shaky, but managing. How's that?"

"Acceptable." Carrington hung on a bit longer. If anything had—no, best not to dwell. His heart hammered in barely leashed, desperate fear over what could have happened. *This hurts, this loving him so much when I'm not always able to keep him safe. I should...though not in front of the parents.* "One of these days, things will be right again. I promise."

"You can't promise that, Carr," Erasmus said in a small voice that nearly broke Carrington's heart.

"The hell I can't," Carrington growled before he moved over to help his mother sit up. "Mom, probably best if you went inside. Please don't look at the garden."

She put a hand to her head. "What's happened here? Carrington, what have you done?"

*Yes, because this is my fault.* "I'll explain in a bit. Can you stand?"

"Yes. I think so." Mom's hesitation was so out of character that Carrington kept a firm grip on her even as she gained her feet.

Dad had managed to get upright on his own. Unfortunately, he faced the garden. "Sweet Jesus, what the devil happened here?"

"Please go inside. I did ask you not to look, Dad."

Placing his feet as if the world might not be quite steady, Dad turned toward the house, shaking his head. "I'm really *very* sorry I did."

Carrington tried to turn his mother toward the house, too, but she planted her feet, glaring out into the dimly lit garden with her arms crossed over her chest. "I don't suppose you've given any thought to who will be cleaning up this mess?"

# Chapter Seven

Jeff had temporarily moved in with Kyle and Kash. When Carrington had called in to report that night, Captain Valbuena had tried to insist that Jeff should stay with him and his rens at the hotel. But the captain did concede that hotel security wasn't as sure as Kash's apartment—well out of range of zorpse activity—and Jeff had objected because he would feel uncomfortable and intrusive living amid what may or may not have been a poly relationship.

"Not to mention, Kash is pretty badass," Jeff had said in a confidential conversation with Carrington before he'd gone out to Kyle's car. "If anyone can hold off zorpses until help gets there, it's him."

The temptation to share that conversation with Captain Valbuena was nearly overwhelming, but Carrington restrained himself. After Pecca's lessons the previous evening, he reasoned the captain's ego was most likely struggling back up the few notches it had been smacked down. Besides, the rens had acted as magical forensics and cleanup for the zorpse remains, so that stood as a mitigating factor.

Mom wasn't happy about the whole thing, especially since she'd been, as she put it, *harboring a criminal all those years*, but at least the Carrington-blaming had subsided by the next morning. He probably shouldn't have suggested that the gore from the remains would be good fertilizer for the lawn.

Uniforms had been sent to Dr. Hayes' house. No one was at all shocked that he wasn't at home or at any of his normal haunts.

"He'll resurface when he's ready for his finale," a grumpy and sleep-deprived Kyle said during roll call that morning.

Lieutenant Dunfee tapped the edges of her papers on the lectern. "No doubt. It's disturbing that he managed to stay hidden for so long, right in plain sight. My apologies to each of you, to your family, Loveless, and to Mr. Graham. I should have picked up on *something* over the years."

"He was our kindly benefactor, ma'am. How would any of us have known?" Carrington scrubbed his hands over his face. "Always there when no one else would help us and it was him setting us up as the pariah precinct all along. If anyone feels duped, it's me. I've known him all my life."

"It's must be hard." Kash's soft voice still managed to carry to the far corners of the room. "I haven't been here as long as most of you, but he fooled me as well. I *liked* talking to him. But I don't suppose that's terribly helpful. We know who. We know something of what. Now we need specifics."

"The only things we know are that Dr. Hayes can summon thespian dead exclusively, that he's planning a larger, more dangerous summoning and that this summoning has to do with fish lords." Carrington surged up from his chair and started pacing when his voice cracked on the last word.

"Oh. *That's* what that meant," Amanda whispered *sotto voce* to Eva.

"Our Mr. Graham heard it too," Kash added. "Willing to bet my right hand that he's already started research."

Carrington stopped his pacing. "Well, yes. He'd already started last night. You can't place mysterious words in front of a librarian and expect him not to."

"Officer Soren's suggesting we provide some help, Loveless." Lieutenant Dunfee's voice was at its flattest. "Take your most likely brains to the library and assist Mr. Graham. Sooner the better."

"Yes, ma'am." Carrington stopped his pacing, blinking at her stupidly. How dense could he be? He'd been trying to approach this as a cop when they needed to approach the problem like librarians.

"Go. Out of my sight. All of you." Lieutenant Dunfee waved a hand in an aggravated gesture. "Lives are depending on us, gods help them."

By the time Carrington had hurried back to the squad room, his brain had re-engaged. "Krisk, do you and Alex have a good handle on Dr. Hayes' scent?"

Krisk nodded and tugged at Alex's sleeve, who added, "Yeah. And what his workings smell like, too."

"Good. I want you searching for him by scent since it's certain he's taken steps not to be seen. Old warehouses, abandoned areas down by the waterfront, anywhere he might have privacy for complex magic." Carrington turned from them and caught Vance by the arm. "You and Amanda go see Pecca, please. She may know what's happened, we have no idea how she gathers intel, but go tell her what we know so far. See if she had any information on these piscatory lords."

The old Vance would have argued and complained. This Vance gave him a sharp nod and turned to call out, "Hey, Manda!"

Carrington continued through the squad room. "Greg, take Kyle for amplification and see what the water folk are saying, if they have any places they're afraid of right now. Shira, Jeremy, you have the squad room. Advise the captain when he calls or comes in. Assist in whatever capacity he requests." Part of him registered the stillness of his squad mates and he had a fleeting vision of them as a quivering hunting pack. *Release the hounds!* "Kash, Jeff, Eva, with me."

"To the Batcave?" Kash asked deadpan.

Carrington mustered up a touch of the theatrical and pointed at the ceiling. "To the library!"

Out in the absurdly bright parking lot, Carrington had a bad moment as he realized he'd sent his regular driver off with Vance, but they soon had things sorted with Eva driving his squad car and Amanda riding shotgun in Vance's, accompanied by a certain amount of grumbling. Amanda could be a terrible passenger.

He took up his regular sunny day position in the car, scrunched down as far as possible, shades on, hat pulled down to meet them.

After a couple of surreptitious side-eyes, Eva asked, "Why don't you get the windows tinted? Regs and all, I know, but you should be able to get a deferral, right?"

"We did try, early on. Apparently, *vampirism* is not on the approved list for tinted windows, even for civilians."

"Everybody thinks being a vampire's so cool. Sounds to me like it sucks." Eva drew in a sharp breath. "Sorry. That wasn't a joke or anything."

"Quite all right. I knew what you meant." Carrington heaved an overdramatic sigh. "Amanda has no qualms about teasing me mercilessly, never fear."

"But you and Manda…you've been partners a long time?"

"We have. She came to the Seventy-Seventh early on when we had no equipment and no real squad. Manda's truly been my rock and who else would put up with my drama and whining?"

Where someone else would have laughed, Eva nodded with her most serious frown. "So…can I ask something personal?"

"You can always ask. If it's not something I'll answer, I'll try to say no politely."

"Fair." Eva drove past the library to find a parking spot. "Does Amanda…? Does she see anyone?"

"Ah, well, that's not a personal question for *me*, so I'm happy to answer." Carrington wiped the smile from his face, since Eva radiated nerves. "Not now, no. She's had girlfriends since I've known her, but they don't tend to last long. Nor are they particularly good for her. The last one threw Manda's stand mixer out the window as part of an art piece. Quotations around the *art* part of that sentence are implied. Then she was amazed when Manda demanded she replace it."

"Ouch. How long ago was that?"

"Let me think…six months? It might be more by now. There hasn't been anyone since." Carrington stole another glance Eva's way and decided to put her out of her misery. "We're not a traditional shop, Eva. I think you know that by now. We've taken the rules about

155

dating fellow officers, strapped them with duct tape and tossed them in the river. Ask Amanda out, if you like. I'd advise a slow approach, but what do I know? My love life was a shambles before Ras. Just don't let personal issues between you creep into work. We take a dark view of that."

"I never said—"

"Yes, yes, I know. I'm being a proactive busybody." Carrington winced as he eased out of the car. It was a good block and a half walk to the library from where Eva had parked. "I'm going to try to make it on my own, but I may need an arm when we get to the library steps."

"I'm not judging, Carr. If you need help, you need help."

He didn't do too badly—all the way to the Shakespeare statue where he made the mistake of tipping his head up to greet Touchstone and Hamlet and looked right into the sun. After leaning against the statue for a good thirty seconds and some creative cussing, he had to admit to Eva that he was effectively blind. Happily, she was an excellent guide and he'd regained everything except full-color spectrum by the time they reached the glass doors to the Rare Books department.

Erasmus hurried down the steps almost as soon as they rang the bell. "Kash and Jeff are up by my desk alrea— Were you looking at the sun?"

"Why would you ask such a thing?" Carrington carefully disengaged his hand from the crook of Eva's arm.

"You're squinty and you have that sort of glassy look."

Carrington threw his hands up in a gesture of despair and appealed to Eva. "Do you see what I have to put up with?"

"Some people would kill to have someone know them that well." Eva's lips compressed as if she were fighting a smile.

"No sympathy at all. Dreadful." Carrington tromped up the stairs, his heart easing to hear the chuckles behind him. There had been far too little laughter in the past few days.

Erasmus jogged around him to get to his desk first, already in full excitable researcher mode. "All right. So I dug through a few things this morning since I'd never heard the term piscatory lords or piscatory anything, actually. What I started with was a book that contains anecdotal cautionary tales addressed to people who want to summon demons. What happens when you break the summoning circle—bad things. What happens when you're unclear about which demon you're summoning—worse things. And then there was an odd, not terribly lucid story about Amin the Mad, who wanted to drown the world and tried to call *creatures from beyond this demesne*. Which couldn't be much vaguer, but it sounds like the right direction for us."

Jeff, who was spinning the silver gyroscope sculpture on Erasmus's desk, asked, "What happened to Amin?"

"Apparently..." Erasmus tugged at his earlobe. "Well, he drowned."

"Wonderful." Carrington clapped his hands together. "We're here to help. Put us where you need us."

The where ended up being one of the climate-controlled reading room with gloves and instructions from Erasmus on how to handle the books. The trail was a faint one and their only instruction was to look for references to poor, drowned Amin.

They'd been at it for hours, each with their own table of books, when Kash finally murmured, "There he is."

Erasmus hurried over. "Oh, yes. Yes, that's him! It's not much, but…" He jogged off again without explanation.

"What does it say?" Carrington leaned across the aisle as if he could read the faded text from six feet away.

"It's not much more than a reference to an old work, *The Compendium of Elrich Manifestations*."

Before long, Erasmus returned with another book, one that appeared newer and was perhaps the thickness of three dictionaries stacked together.

"Just like that? You have this compendium?" Carrington fought to bring his rising brows under control.

"No, it's not usually that simple. But this book, *A Collection of Occult Lore*, probably has passages about it and maybe even from it."

It took some searching, both in the index and in listings from sources online, but Erasmus tracked down the entry, never tiring, constantly muttering to himself. "Here. This is what is says about Amin the Mad. *The several apprentices begged their master not to engage in this perilous working, but Amin would not be dissuaded. A virgin was procured and sacrificed to the foul summoning and when Amin chanted the prescribed words, the sky cracked open and they espied horrors within, demons of fearsome oceanic aspect. One of the demons reached a foul appendage through and touched it to Amin and a man no longer stood in his place. His visage was scaled and his eyes bulbous as a carp. He gasped with lungs no longer suited to air and died.*"

After a stunned silence, Carrington murmured, "That's rather the reverse of drowning."

"It's horrible is what it was," Eva murmured. "So the fish lords come through the crack in reality and turn people into fish?"

"That seems to be part of it, but Amin must've done something wrong in the spell. I'm sure that's not the outcome he wanted." Erasmus went right back to searching.

Jeff cleared his throat. "I don't suppose anyone noticed the whole *sacrifice the virgin to open the sky* part?"

"Yes. Just another reason to stop him before he has a chance to start the summoning." Kash fell silent, staring at the desk.

"There's something in here about drowning the world," Eva said after she'd searched her own book a few minutes more. "City by city. Look. The illustration. The waters are coming up to the tops of the towers and the people are turning into fish."

Carrington glanced over her shoulder at the crude illustration. Terrible grasp of perspective and proportion or not, people were definitely turning into fish. "Lovely. Though it does clarify his statements about remaking the world."

"And he couldn't have found a different sacrifice?" Jeff sat back, arms crossed over his chest. "I can't *possibly* be the only virgin in the city."

Eva frowned hard at him. "Can't you...? I mean, there's things you could do to not be a virgin."

"No. Sorry. Hard no on that." Jeff held up a hand. "Look, I know some asexual people are okay with sex, but I'm not one of them. Touch is great, but once you start getting into mouths on things and putting nether parts together, I just can't."

"Sorry." Eva's frown reached up to crease her forehead. "I didn't know you were ace."

Jeff shrugged. "Not exactly something that comes up at work very often."

"In an attempt to answer Jeff's question" — Carrington leaned back against one of the reading tables, then thought better of it when it shifted under him — "I think that has to do with Dr. Hayes' rather complicated relationship to the squad."

"Sort of a *he created you, and now you're going to help complete his purpose* kind of thinking thing?" Erasmus closed the Compendium. "That's not crazy at all."

"The whole thing's quite a few rail stops away from sane," Kash offered softly. "But I think Carr's right. He seems to feel a certain ownership. Probably resentment, too."

"For us meddling kids always ruining his plans? I can see that." Jeff closed his eyes with a tired sigh. "I hope this is our last evil genius ever."

Kash closed his book and returned it to the cart Erasmus had used to bring the books out. "I wonder what they've promised him. The demon lords always make promises they don't intend to keep."

Carrington raised an eyebrow at him. "I don't want to know what you've been reading lately. We need to regroup and have a war council. Then, we need to find him."

"It's a good thing we're used to doing seventeen impossible things before breakfast." Kash gave him a hint of a smile, still serene despite everything. For whatever obscure reason, that settled Carrington's nerves.

"Truer words," Carrington said with a sharp laugh. "All right, let's get back and call in the troops. As Ms. Pecca has said more than once, I think we're running out of time for—"

"Let me put the books away and I'll come with you," Erasmus broke in.

Carrington crossed the floor to him and caught one of his hands. "Ras, no. You've helped so much and it's wonderful that you want to help. But this? This is too dan—"

"Don't." Erasmus pointed a finger in his face. "Don't you dare say it. If you think I'm too dense to understand that your job is *dangerous* by now, I don't know why you're with me. Believe me, I know. Every time you walk out the damn door to go to work, I fight myself thinking about it and trying not to think about it. Wondering if this is the time you don't walk back through that door at the end of shift. If this is the time I get the phone call. Don't you think I don't know?"

"I never—" Carrington struggled to put words together in the face of this fierce and unexpected assault. "I know that you know. And that's not at all what I wanted to imply. You're right. This is my job. It's what I do. For me to put you in dangerous situations, though, to knowingly place you in peril? It's not *your* job. You didn't sign up for that."

Erasmus took his hand back and started putting the antique books back on his cart. For a moment, Carrington sagged in relief, assuming that Erasmus had acquiesced.

That lasted approximately ten seconds until Erasmus said, "You can leave me behind, but I'll be following. I'm part of this, Carr—part of this case, part of this city, part of this relationship. Hell if I'm going to sit by and wonder if I'm going to be a fish by morning."

"We may need every mind and every magic user in our reach," Kash added.

"Wonderful. Ganging up on me." Carrington snorted when he found he was out of arguments. "Fine. Meet us at the precinct. But if you die, so help me, I'll never forgive you."

Erasmus gave him an almost-smile. "I'll be sure to haunt you so you can yell at me."

"Please do." Carrington gave him a quick kiss and strode out of the room before he made a fool of himself. *More of a fool.*

He'd almost made it down the stairs in the entrance hall when a long hand landed on his shoulder.

"I know, Carr," Kash said in his smooth, soft tones. "Believe me, I know. I almost lost Kyle to a panicked pill bug and an ichthyosaur."

"I do recall." Carrington looked up into sympathetic blue eyes. "How do you keep your heart from cracking?"

Kash gave a last pat and continued down the stairs. "I don't. Kyle has to help me put the pieces back every time it cracks."

"Comforting," Carrington grumbled as he continued down the stairs.

\* \* \* \*

Back at the precinct, the troops were already gathering and Captain Valbuena's shining black State Paranormal van was pulling into the parking lot to lord it over the more pedestrian black-and-whites.

"Greg, anything?" Carrington wasted no time as soon as he strode into the squad room.

"Nothing specific." Greg looked up from his computer screen. "The ducks and the seagulls are scared, but they weren't thinking about a specific place."

"Seemed worse on the Schuylkill side than the Delaware side. Hard to tell," Kyle added with a shudder. "Duck feelings are weird."

"You get used to them."

That did point to Dr. Hayes not returning to the waterfront, though, which might narrow the search down a fingernail-width. It made sense since Kash had destroyed his last place of sorcerous working in the abandoned power plant. Unlikely that he would return to the same area.

Carrington turned to the other side of the room. "Alex?"

Krisk thumped his tail in an irritable rhythm and by the drawing down of Alex's shaggy eyebrows, he wasn't any happier. "We found trails, Carr. Problem is he's everywhere and really hard to track because the trails overlap. Some are old and too faded. Some are newer, but didn't lead us anywhere."

"Thank you for trying. It was worth a shot." Carrington turned again, feeling like a wooden top by now, as Erasmus came in from the front hall. "Ras."

"Gonna tell me to go?"

Carrington shook his head, though that crack in his heart was expanding. "No. Stay. I—I'm sorry."

"Don't be, hon." Erasmus came and kissed his cheek. "Not now, anyway. Maybe later."

The vibration against his leg was ill-timed, but Amanda was calling. "Are you on your way?"

"Coming to you, Carr. Pecca's with us." Amanda hesitated as someone spoke in the background. "She wants to talk to Hunter when she gets there."

"Very good. We'll let her know."

Carrington had just tucked the phone away when the Royal Vampire Guard trooped in pushing Captain Valbuena's traveling box. Mina locked the wheels while the others undid the latches and helped a somewhat rumpled and singed-around-the-ears vampire captain down from his container.

"Captain? Everything all right?" Carrington strode over, making sure to keep enough distance that the rens wouldn't mistake his approach for threat display. They seemed more experienced than that, but he'd seen more than one ren take down someone else's vamp at State for nothing more than walking up too fast.

"Your necromancer has been active far longer than I feared." Captain Valbuena scowled at a dust smudge on his sleeve and made a futile attempt to brush it off. "We found no less than seven old sites where he'd engaged in workings. Some as many as twenty years ago. The man does seem to like crumbling buildings, I will say that."

"No sign of his current site?"

Valbuena glared as if the question had been a personal insult, then he slumped and waved a hand in a frustrated gesture. "No. At some point, oh, perhaps ten years ago, he began to experiment with obscuring his magical signature. Not always successfully, but he's had time to perfect it."

"Thank you for trying, sir. We're not out of options quite yet." *Hunter. I need to find Hunter.* "Excuse me a moment, sir."

Carrington checked under Alex's desk, in case Hunter was hanging out with Audacity, but the space was empty. He peered into the gloom of the half-lit breakroom next. It was deserted. Finally, he went back to LJ and Hunter's room and knocked on the door.

"LJ? Hunter? Are you all right in there?"

Rustling came from within, then LJ opened the door. Hunter huddled on the bed, sleeves wrapped around her body as she rocked miserably. LJ gestured to her, then out toward the squad room, and finally made a circling motion that appeared to encompass everything.

"Hunter believes this is all her fault?" Carrington guessed. When LJ gave a collar nod, he pushed through to kneel by the bed. "Hunter, don't think that way. This man has been making and revising plans for twenty years, at least. That's longer than we've been in this building and I'd be willing to wager longer than you've existed as you."

Hunter shrugged and wiped at nonexistent eyes.

"Maybe he's used you in some terrible way. We don't know yet. Even if he has, that's not your fault. Do you hear me? You're not responsible for his evil." Carrington waited for her tiny nod before he went on. "Pecca's coming. She wants to talk to you. If you can help—help us stop him, help us keep Jeff safe and save the city—don't you want to?"

Her next nod was definite, close to fierce, and LJ swooped in to hug her tight.

"Take a moment to compose yourself before you come out into the squad room. We're going to need everyone on this, I think."

She nodded again around LJ and held up a sleeve with the cuff pinched at the top—most likely a Hunter version of a thumbs-up. By the level of conversation coming from the squad room, Amanda had arrived with Pecca and Vance. Carrington hurried back out with the sincere hope that everyone was going to gather in one room now and he could stop running back and forth.

It didn't escape his attention that Pecca was holding Vance's hand and didn't show any indication of letting go. Vance was a little red around the ears, probably not entirely comfortable with handholding in the squad room. Calling it out would've drawn more attention to it, so Carrington decided to ignore the inappropriate display.

"Ms. Pecca, Hunter will be right out." *She's just having a bit of a coat cry.*

"Good, good." Pecca let go of Vance, patted Captain Valbuena's chest absently and began wandering the squad room, gaze flicking here and there.

"Are you...looking for something?" Carrington asked after a few baffled moments.

She nodded, maybe to herself, and kept wandering. Past Greg and Shira's joined desk she whirled and came back. "Yes. Yes. Looking. Officer Amanda told me about the cufflink." She got on her hands and knees to peer at the underside of Greg's desk. "Probably really upset when another police department took it. He wanted it here to — aha!"

With a triumphant wave, she popped back up to her feet with a thumbnail-sized object held in her hand.

"What is it?" Carrington hurried to her, sliding through his squad mates who were crowding around.

Pecca held her hand out to show him. A metal skull nestled in her palm, smaller than Dr. Hayes' cufflink had been, though the design was nearly identical, platinum with diamond chips for eyes. Carrington took it from Pecca and she went back to searching.

By the time she declared the room swept, four little skulls lay lined up on Greg's desk.

"Listening devices?" Kash asked as he examined them.

Pecca laid a finger to her lips, which answered the question for Carrington, and before anyone else could give anything more away, she clapped her hands twice. The skulls crumbled into dust.

"Yes. He has been listening." Pecca gestured toward Hunter, who had just floated into the room. "But not through any coats or jackets."

"Damn him," Kyle spat out. "He planted them the times he visited here."

"It's all been so purposeful," Erasmus said in his thinking voice. "He wanted you to figure it all out."

Shira peered at the platinum dust. "You think he wanted to be caught?"

"I think he wanted someone to know," Carrington said with growing certainty. He reached for the nearest chair and sat hard. "I think he wanted *me* to know. He's used me all along."

"You better not be blaming yourself, Carr. He created a bad situation. We've all done the best we could with it." Jeff leaned on the desk beside him. "Why couldn't any of us sense magical listening devices, Ms. Pecca? Why couldn't Alex or Krisk *smell* them?"

"He's made being invisible into an art," Pecca answered. "I'd admire what he's done if it wasn't all evil stuff. Remember that he fooled me too when he gave me the animal book. I couldn't tell what he looked like and I was standing right there, chatting with him."

Vance cleared his throat. "If he can always hide himself, how do we find him?"

"His working, his great work, will reveal him." Pecca held out a hand to Hunter. "But by then it could be too late. Hunter, you were his. And sometimes, threads remain."

Once, Carrington wouldn't have known what she was on about. Now, he had a good inkling. A shiver ran through him and he glanced out the windows. Full dark. The sun had set, as it had a habit of doing every day. Normally, he welcomed the night. This night gave him a Terrible Feeling.

Hunter hovered as still as she could while Pecca ran her hands through the air around her, humming. Slender silken threads of light began to shimmer around Hunter—maybe her life force or her visible connection to the universe. Carrington didn't have the vocabulary for it yet. One thicker, bright green strand linked to LJ, which wasn't surprising. Other paler strands connected to the rest of the people in the room, to Audacity, now perched on her Dad's shoulder, to Edgar, sulking on his perch, and even to Tim, who had just rolled out of the breakroom.

One was different. A faded gray thread ran from Hunter's center and didn't connect to anything in the room. It ran out of the window and into the night.

Pecca pointed to it. "Can everyone see that?" Kash, Vance and Ras nodded, everyone else had puzzled expressions. "There's our connection. He hasn't been able to use Hunter as he'd probably hoped to. But we can follow that thread back."

Amanda stood from her slouch against Kyle's desk. "Let's go, then. What're we d—"

Lieutenant Dunfee's door flew open with a crash. "Too late. He's here. I'm holding the front door, but they're surrounding the building."

*Damn it. Always one step behind.* Captain Valbuena zipped to the front door as only a full vampire could, presumably to lock it, as the lieutenant caught herself on the doorframe.

"Watch the windows," she called out in a ragged voice. "We're about to be besieged. Edgar!"

"Fuck, fuck, fuckity fuck fuck fucknuckle!" Edgar screamed as he left his perch in a blue and pink surge of feathers and flew to Lieutenant Dunfee's shoulder.

"Source. Her source," Erasmus murmured as he took Carrington's hand.

"Maker, conduit, source!" Pecca called out, her thoughts obviously paralleling Erasmus' as she rushed around the room and placed people in triads, facing them towards one bank of windows or another. "Captain, do your people have magic?"

"No, but they have weapons."

"Good. Come and join Officer Vampire and Mr. Graham. You three will be *formidable.*"

She lined them up and had them face the front hall, and Carrington had to assume her thinking mirrored his. That old door would only hold so long.

"LJ!" Carrington called out. They needed a place for non-combatants that didn't have windows. "Take Audacity, Hunter and Tim to your room and lock the door!"

Erasmus twitched as the first zorpse slammed into one of the west-facing windows. A muted crowd murmur reached Carrington's ears from the shouted theatrical lines. Hard to tell with the lights on in the squad room, but the murmur was more of an ocean than a stream of words.

"It's a few more than eight this time," he said for his triad's ears alone.

"Quite," Captain Valbuena said in a dry tone, then raised his voice. "Mina! Kadan! Sean! Officer Krisk! Protect Officer Gatling! Yvon! Javier! Hold that front hall! Nothing gets through!"

The rens moved without hesitation, the only sounds from them the slaps of heavy boots running across the floorboards and the snicks and clacks of weapons drawn and at the ready.

"I can help, you know," Jeff objected with a touch of heat. The rens showed sense and backed off far enough to give him a clear shot with his revolver.

"We aim for the heads, ma'am, like in the movies?" Greg asked from where he had one hand on the lieutenant's shoulder as her conduit and the other on his handgun.

"Just like in the movies, Santos," Lieutenant Dunfee answered. "Probably best to pretend you're in one."

A second and third zorpse smashed into the windows. The panes shuddered as more zorpses lurched out of the night to add their mindless smashing. Their shouted lines from Eugene O'Neill, Sarah Kane, Clare Booth Luce and so on were finally discernible through the windows.

Their delivery was terrible. Their diction worse.

"Coming through on our side!" Vance bellowed.

A spine-piercing shriek of glass came on the heel of his words, then a horrific shattering as half the panes in the center west window crashed down. The horde of zorpses reached inside and began to pull themselves in, heedless of the broken glass and what they might leave behind.

Vance's yell conveyed as much fear as bravado as he pulled power from Amanda through Shira. A fireball exploded from his outstretched hand, bigger than the desks it hurtled over, and Carrington feared they would die of self-immolation rather than zorpse attack. But Vance held tight control of that screaming bit of pyrotechnics. It singed the broken window frame but didn't ignite the walls. When the blaze cleared, that window was empty.

Not that it would be the case for long.

The coffeemaker sailed from the counter to take out the one zorpse that had gotten in before Vance's fireball — Larry the ghost showing his displeasure at having his squad room invaded.

Weapons fire sounded in the front hallway. Their besiegers had broken through the front door, but the rens held position so the zorpses weren't getting far. The window nearest Lieutenant Dunfee splintered and cascaded to the floor in sections.

"Fuck you and the ass-faced hippo you rode in on!" Edgar shrieked as the lieutenant raised a hand toward the lurching undead thespians.

The surge of power she drew rumbled through the floor. Greg's complexion grayed as it flooded through him but he held fast. No visible bolts of magic flew from Lieutenant Dunfee, though. They manifested as shockwaves hitting one zorpse after another, and everywhere those waves hit, a zorpse head exploded. *Good thing. They were mangling Wilde.*

"Ours is going next," Captain Valbuena murmured. "Stand ready."

Half a second later, their window caved under the pressure of the mass of zorpses. Captain Valbuena drew a long breath, Carrington tried to relax into the heavy-handed pull of power, and the captain got off a bolt of lightning that split the lead zorpse's head in two.

His second bolt flew —

A shockwave like a giant hand smashed into Carrington and lifted him from his feet. He had time to clutch Ras to him hard and to realize that all the lights had blown out before he hit something unyielding and went out himself.

Several moments or hours later, Carrington woke in an excruciating semi-upside-down position crumpled between the wall and Ras. The lights in the squad room were on again and while it wasn't quiet, no more shouted lines from disconnected plays came through the windows.

He righted himself carefully and made sure Erasmus was waking up as well before he took stock. Only Lieutenant Dunfee and Pecca were on their feet, going from officer to officer to check their status. Captain Valbuena was completing a crawl across the floor to where one of his rens sprawled.

"Kadan?" The captain's voice shook and Carrington might not have liked the man, but it still pierced his heart to hear it. "Kadan!"

"Should be okay, sir." Mina was there immediately with a hand on his arm. "He's breathing fine."

"All right. Yes." Captain Valbuena's hard swallow was audible across the room. "Where's Officer Gatling?"

Carrington used the wall to lever himself up for a better view of the room. All of his officers, yes, except...

"Jeff's gone." His chest felt hollow as he repeated it louder. "Jeff's gone."

"Thank you, Officer Obvious," the lieutenant grumbled from across the room. "We're going after him as soon as I have enough of a force standing. Are you fit?"

"Yes, ma'am. Waiting to see on Ras."

"Fine. I'm fine," Erasmus said from the floor. "Good gods, what happened?"

Lieutenant Dunfee's tone was sharper than normal as she said, "Dr. Hayes got impatient. He hit us with something that knocked us flat and took out a number of his minions. But it accomplished what he wanted and now he has Gatling."

Krisk was up and about, pacing. He disappeared into the breakroom for a few moments, probably to get some water since he dehydrated easily. Soon enough he was back, though, patting his jacket pockets and looking ready for anything.

"He's gonna kill Jeff," Vance whispered, his shaking radiating from across the room. "He's gonna kill Jeff and feed him to fish gods."

"Shh." Pecca hopped over people still trying to sit up to reach him. "Vance, fields. Soft light. Deep breath." She took his face between her hands and he stilled, eyes wide. "Breathe with me. Breathe. I'm the only one in the room right now. Do you see me?"

"Yeah." Vance's voice was soft, steadier.

"Good. We're going to go save Jeff. If you don't think you're going to be all right, you need to stay here."

"Fuck that. Um, sorry, Ms. Pecca. I'm mean I'm coming with. For Jeff saving."

Interesting as it was to watch Pecca corral Vance's PTSD—and it *was* fascinating—they had to move.

Every second was going to count. Nearly everyone had managed at least a sitting position by now, even Kadan.

"Who's fit to drive?" Lieutenant Dunfee barked out.

Mina raised her hand, Carrington, his, then Greg.

"All right, let's load up, people. Captain, your van in the lead with Teecosi in the front seat with Hunter. Load up as many of my people as you can. Loveless, Krisk and Wolf with you and Zacchini. Mr. Graham won't take up much room. No, Tim, you can't go. Find somewhere to hide for now."

Audacity had come out from under something and was dancing in front of the lieutenant, meowing insistently.

"Damn it, no, Cadet. You can*not* come along on this. Children don't belong in a firefight."

"Go hide with Tim, sweetie," Wolf said as he clutched his head in both hands. "I'd take you home to Grandma, but we don't have time."

Audacity plunked down on the floor, clearly sulking, but she gave up her argument. There was a good deal of lurching as they left the building in an imitation of zorpses. Kyle was dazed and had to be turned three times before he was moving in the right direction to get in the back of Greg's squad car.

Carrington took position behind the van, with the lieutenant directly behind him and Greg following. If he squinted, he could just make out the gray thread Pecca followed as they careened down side streets and made unexpected sharp turns at her direction. Hunter had to be scared half to death, but unlike certain past incidents, she didn't attempt a jump and run.

He'd expected the trail to lead to some out-of-the-way abandoned industrial site, but the neighborhoods became more and more familiar as they drove. They were headed to Dr. Hayes' house.

Inside? It had been a few years since he'd been to the cute little Tudor cottage tucked behind a screen of old pines and hemlocks. Inside didn't seem likely. The house wasn't a sprawling pile and the rooms were cozy and intimate. Not well suited to interdimensional summoning.

Outside, though...

Carrington veered onto the shoulder and floored it, overtaking the more ponderous van and cutting it off at the end of the long drive. He leaped out and dashed to the driver's side, where Mina rolled the window down and regarded him with the same professional disinterest she showed to everyone but the captain.

"I know this house. It's his. I used to come here often with my parents. There's a little knoll in the garden. The highest point on the property." Carrington gestured toward the back of the house. "Better to leave the cars and go around the left side of the house where we'll be less visible. There's a flat space at the top of the knoll, encircled by stone benches. If a summoning were to take place anywhere, it would be there."

Mina turned toward the back of the van. "Sir?"

"Trust the man who knows the terrain," Captain Valbuena's voice drifted from the interior.

She threw the van into park and immediately officers, civilians and entities poured from four vehicles.

Pecca still held Hunter's sleeve, though she released it with a pat. "Stay here, coatfriends. Don't let him see you. If we fail... We'll do our best to not do that, but if we do, run fast and far."

Lieutenant Dunfee reached them with Edgar perched on her shoulder. "Captain, I suggest we form up now into triads. No scrambling when we get there. Krisk, I'm putting you with the rens for perimeter guard. No doubt he has minions to keep us away from his working."

"He knows we're coming?" Greg whispered.

"There's no conceivable way he's missed our arrival," she said with a snort. "Probably even anticipating it."

"I agree. Loveless, Mr. Graham, with me then." Captain Valbuena turned to his troops. "Kadan? You're up for this?"

The young man in question tucked a lock of hair back that had come out of the captain's usually neat tail. "I'm fine, sir. You be careful."

All of his rens touched him before they fanned out to take point and Mina even tugged him down for a quick kiss. Heartwarming, yes, but to Carrington, the open show of affection was far more ominous than touching. They didn't expect to come out of this alive.

As ordered, they grouped in triads — Greg and Edgar with the lieutenant, Kyle and Eva with Kash, Shira and Amanda with Vance, and Wolf and Jeremy with Pecca. As they moved out, staying off the gravel driveway to minimize noise, Carrington took a quick glance back at Hunter and LJ. They held each other tight — strange orphans abandoned on the darkest possible of nights. LJ lifted a sleeve in a wave and Carrington returned it with a salute. They were, without a doubt, the bravest jackets he had ever met.

As they rounded the house, a glow became visible through the screen of willows in front of them. Hard to make anything out yet since the willows stubbornly held onto some of their foliage still, rustling irritably in the night breeze, tossing the long fingers of their leaves into the decorative pond at their center, and obscuring the knoll. The charge of magic was unmistakable, seen or not. Dr. Hayes had already begun.

When they pushed through the branches, Carrington's heart gave a painful thud. Dr. Hayes stood in the middle of the stone circle, the stone table before him a feature of the knoll that Carrington knew hadn't been there before. A corpse-white glow emanated from both the benches and the table and in this sickly light lay Jeff, strapped down spread eagle and stripped to the waist, with blood pooling at his side. For one horrible moment, Carrington believed he was dead. Then Jeff yanked at the thick leather securing his wrists and said something Carrington couldn't quite catch.

"Don't worry, my dear. It won't take long at all," Dr. Hayes replied as he finished setting candles at five points along the circle. "Mostly painless, I'm sure. Terribly sorry about the blood, but it's necessary for the spell, you see. And your friends are here. Now you needn't feel so awfully alone."

The time for stealth at an end, Carrington waved to the other teams to surround the position and strode out of the willow grove to stand at the foot of the knoll. "Dr. Hayes, this hasn't ended well for previous practitioners."

"Hello, my boy. Nice to see you here. You haven't been to visit me in such a long time. Busy, I suppose." Dr. Hayes lit bunches of herbs on the altar, since what else could one call it? "This really is for the best. Have faith that I've done my research and have completed negotiations."

"To what end, sir? The Piscatory Lords will drown the city. We'll all be fish and so will you. Then what? It's one city in this whole, rotten world."

"It is. It is indeed. You won't be a fish, per se. That's an error on the part of earlier researchers. The humans within the city limits will become fish *people*, though I'm afraid you'll lose a good portion of your intellect. Rather a shame about that." Dr. Hayes moved his hands through the smoke, creating intricate patterns. "Your parents never gave you enough credit. Smart as a whip, even as a child. Ah, well. What the old accounts don't tell you is that once the Piscatory Lords claim this city, it becomes... I suppose you might use the word *infected*. Anyone entering the borders of the spell will change and anyone who leaves will change those with whom they have contact. The waters will rise and cause neighboring waters to rise in answer. It will spread and soon we will have Washington. From there, everything becomes absurdly easy."

"But you'll lose your intellectual capacity as well, as a fish person. It sounds like the whole thing will be out of your hands and who knows what marine beings from another plane really want?"

"Ah, and that's why negotiations with summoned beings are so important." Dr. Hayes smiled. "I won't be a fish. I will be granted the aspect of cephalopod, and so retain my intellectual prowess. You may want to warn your friends that there are undead actors about to surround them."

"They know. I wish it had been someone else, sir."

"Now, now. Anyone else would have wanted some odd version of power. Better that it's me. No more war or poverty. No racism or conflicts of religion or destruction of the environment."

"I'm sorry, Dr. Hayes." Carrington pulled his weapon, aimed and fired, hoping to end everything in an expedient, non-cinematic way. The bullet, naturally, ricocheted off an invisible barrier and forced Carrington to crouch or be taken out by his own shot.

Dr. Hayes *tsked*. "All this preparation. I would hardly neglect personal safety."

"It was worth a try." Carrington kept his handgun out since shots sounded from the trees. The rens had engaged the zorpses, apparently. No telling how many of them yet. He twitched when a hand landed on his shoulder, but Erasmus' scent prevented a more drastic reaction.

"Carr, the lieutenant has the makers on one radio frequency. We're following Pecca's lead."

Ras spoke close to his ear as Captain Valbuena joined them. Pecca's group had emerged from the trees on their right, Lieutenant Dunfee's on their left. He had to assume Kash and Vance's were on the far side of the knoll.

The rate of gunfire increased, the rens obviously using larger bore weapons than police-issue handguns. Carrington placed himself on the outside of their triad as Dr. Hayes began to chant in an unintelligible, gurgling language.

"Captain, advise the others to put their armed sources or conduits on the outside, please. There will be zorpses breaking through the line," Carrington called back.

At any other time, Carrington would have been shocked when the captain complied without argument, but there was no time for shock now. "And tell them to be careful," he concluded in his instructions to the other makers through the radio. "My people and Officer Krisk will be moving faster than those…zorpses. But be sure of your shots."

A sharp wind rose, frigid and moaning. Branches cracked and fell with bone-shaking crashes from the old-growth trees behind the house. *Yes, because we needed another hazard.* Leaves and twigs bounced off the walls Dr. Hayes had thrown up around his working, though the quick glance Carrington risked showed that the walls were exclusively vertical. Somewhere above their heads, the magical field ended since a few leaves did swirl down from the top.

In a horrible way, it made sense, since the fish lords would need access to their sacrifice.

The captain's radio squawked and Pecca's voice came through. "We need to break his fortress. Anything you can do to bring the wall down!"

Carrington planted his feet as he faced the trees, preparing for the heavy pull of magic. Erasmus' hand trembled on his shoulder, probably mostly shivering. Poor Ras didn't have enough meat on his bones and wasn't dressed for the biting wind. Without taking his eyes off the tree line, Carrington shrugged out of his jacket and handed it back, absurdly pleased when Ras took it.

Flame roared on the other side of the knoll, a bright flare lighting up the trees. *That's Vance.* The ground rumbled and something gave with a sharp crack. *And that would be Kash.* Carrington gritted his teeth as Captain Valbuena gathered power in a hard surge. He *felt* the captain's lightning bolts through Ras before they flashed behind him, but so far Dr. Hayes hadn't even hesitated in his chanting.

A strange hum undercut the wind, followed by a crackling that pulled the hair on the back of Carrington's neck on end. He twisted for a quick check and wished he hadn't. The sky was ripping, a jagged tear of misty gray slowly elongating against the deep blue of the normal autumn night. Perspective was tricky, but it appeared to form directly above the knoll—directly above Jeff.

Shockwaves, fire, lightning and storm pummeled the magic defense wall, the crashes and explosions so loud that Carrington almost missed the scuff of leaves from the nearby trees. Two zorpses had slipped by their outer perimeter, heading for him. Carrington raised his weapon in both hands, steadying himself so he wouldn't jar Ras too much, and fired. The first shot hit the left side of the zorpse's face, in the middle of its St. Crispin's Day speech. Two more shots and the thing still came on. Carrington had to empty the entire magazine before it would stay down. *Well, hell and damnation. This won't do.*

"Carr!" Alex roared from his right.

He took his eyes off the advancing zorpses long enough to catch the heavy oak branch Alex tossed him. A regular human would never have been able to throw it so casually and would've been knocked flat trying to catch it. In Carrington's hands, it felt perfect.

He flashed Alex a fanged grin. "Thank you!"

It didn't make him happy to let the zorpses get so close, but he swung hard at the next one to approach and knocked its decaying head clean off. *Ah, yes. Much better.*

He found a rhythm as more zorpses broke through. *Swing, crunch, snap.* Rather satisfying in a dreadful, morbid way. But there were so *many* of them.

Carrington found a moment to yell, "Captain, we're getting a lot of unfriendlies back here!"

"Mina! Status!" Captain Valbuena barked into his radio.

"We're all still up and shooting, sir!" Mina's voice crackled and broke through the steady gunfire. Her next words conveyed undisguised contempt. "Officer Krisk just turned tail and ran, though!"

"What? No!" Carrington shouted, though no one had time to argue with him. Mina had to be mistaken. Krisk was one of the bravest people he'd ever met. Though, perhaps, his people had encountered the fish lords before and had developed a species-deep fear of them.

Pecca's voice held an edge of desperation over the radio. "Concentrate on holding Officer Gatling! We can't let him go through that crack! Think of pulling down! Heavy weight! Don't let him go!"

"Oh gods," Ras whispered and Carrington was compelled to look.

The top of the stone table, with Jeff on it, was rising toward the widening crack in the sky. Jeff struggled wildly, but couldn't get any leverage against the thick leather holding him.

"Any day now, folks! I'd be happy with a rescue anytime here, really! Not picky about the method, either!" Jeff's words were probably partly bravado, partly an attempt to distract Dr. Hayes. The attempt had no effect on Dr. Hayes' chanting, though. He kept right on going, oblivious to Jeff, magic attacks or the continued decimation of his undead army.

The stone table wobbled as various magic users turned their attention on it. Its rate of ascent slowed but didn't stop. Dr. Hayes' chanting grew louder, faster. The crack in the sky opened wide enough to show glimpses of gigantic bulbous eyes and unclassifiable, undulating appendages.

Carrington had to turn back to his zorpse spattering as three of them shambled within clubbing distance. It was exhausting, splitting his attention between trying to keep attackers back and fighting against closing off his magic reservoir.

"I'm not getting enough to pull the stone down!" the captain finally bellowed in frustration. "We're losing him!"

Carrington had cleared the lawn in front of him and called back, "I'm not sure what you want me to do, Captain! Manning two fronts here!"

"Hey." Ras spoke in his ear so he didn't have to shout. "You're doing amazing. But you're, well, clenching up."

"I'm what?"

"Closing off the valve. Carr, you have to open the channels like you did at Pecca's house."

"Surrender."

"Yes. You have to trust me and let go. The captain's not the best at this yet, but I won't let him hurt you."

*Trust.* Carrington stared into those sincere, dark eyes and swallowed hard. "I love you, you know."

Ras squinted at him. "Seriously, Loveless? You're going to pull that out *now* of all places?"

"But…I do love you."

"I know." Ras gave him a soft cuff to the shoulder. "Now concentrate."

Carrington couldn't afford to close his eyes as he'd done in practice. Instead, he concentrated on the beautiful hand on his shoulder, the warmth at his back, the love that danced in the streams of magic every time he and Ras shared power. He kept an eye on the trees, but let himself fall into the question of his lover's tidal pull.

Surrender, complete and utter, with the magic flowing outward from every nerve and fiber of him, a steady outpouring he could almost *see* as Ras gathered it in, gently, oh so gently and passed it on faster, brighter, stronger than what he took.

"Yes!" Captain Valbuena's cry teetered between triumph and ecstasy.

Carrington had a flash of sight through the captain's eyes as the table's ascent halted and after a wobbling struggle, reversed. The descent was agonizingly slow, though, and the things on the other side of the dimensional crack had begun to take an interest, slick tendril appendages reaching tentatively across into the human world.

Doggedly, Carrington took out the next zorpse who came for them, this one spouting lines from *Lysistrata*. They didn't have the training or the firepower to combat a necromancer with decades of practice. They were going to lose and the world would drown. But he sure as hell wasn't going down chewed on by some resurrected actor who couldn't even pronounce Calonice.

Movement above him snagged his attention, his heart hammering with the possibility of a second crack opening. No. No, this movement was something flying above the trees. A night bird? An impossibly large bat?

Carrington had just settled on 'drone' when the object whizzed by above his head. It was LJ with Hunter close behind, and oh, gods of night, LJ held Audacity in his sleeves. *I hope Alex didn't see —*

"Audi, no!" Alex bellowed, though he couldn't race after them with his body caught in the chain of source-conduit-maker.

They flew on, over the top of the magic defense wall. Krisk barreled out of the trees with what appeared to be a long piece of pipe and something white clutched in his right hand. When LJ reached the center of the circle, just above Dr. Hayes, he swooped down and deposited Audacity atop the necromancer's head.

The howl from Alex was so heart-stopping in its grief, several zorpses collapsed under the weight of it. Audacity didn't allow it to distract her, though. She dug her claws in and clung to Dr. Hayes' skull, wailing and shrieking, clinging like a particularly sharp limpet no matter how much he whirled and clutched at her.

While he screamed, face turned up as he tried to dislodge the ninja kitten, Hunter dropped something into his open mouth. He choked and coughed, then began to spit.

"No! No, you can't do this!"

LJ dropped more of the white substance in his eyes and Dr. Hayes' shriek sliced across every other sound. He scrabbled at his face, turning and bellowing spell phrases, while Audacity leaped from his head and ran down the hill.

*Down. The. Hill.*

No sooner had Carrington realized that the defense wall had broken than Krisk charged *up* the hill. He slammed Dr. Hayes to the dirt, shoved the pipe in his mouth and dumped an entire quart bag of white down the pipe. Salt, Carrington realized. It was *salt*. The conversation at the reception came back to him – Dr. Hayes saying he'd had to give up salt entirely. It hadn't been for his health. It had been for necromantic purification. Even the most novice necromancers knew they couldn't work their brand of spells if they'd consumed salt.

Dr. Hayes bucked and choked, his face turning an amazing shade of puce, but he couldn't overpower Krisk. The stone tabletop slammed back down on its supports. Krisk left the writhing necromancer to roll in agony in the dirt and leaped to the table, where he slashed the leather bindings apart with his claws. Sickening gray appendages reached for him through the crack in the sky. Krisk hissed at them, gathered Jeff in his arms and was off the hill in four bounds, leaving the fish lords grasping at nothing.

Perhaps not entirely nothing.

They peered through the crack and focused on Dr. Hayes, blinded and choking beside the altar. He cleared his eyes just in time to see those glistening tendrils reaching toward him.

"We had a pact! You can't do this!" He edged away, trying to rise, but it was obvious he'd started moving too late. "We had an agreement! No! No!"

The tendrils touched his face and arms in a terrible parody of a lover's caress. The scream wrenched from Dr. Hayes was one of pure terror and despair. With a last gasp of escaping breath, he cried out, "Someone feed the gouramis!"

In an eerie flash of light, he was gone. The remaining zorpses fell where they stood, still and peaceful in death once more.

The rip in the universe, however, did not have the decency to vanish.

Pecca's shout came through breathless and desperate. "Close the sky! We have to close the sky! Think closed, closed, closed!"

The fish lords had clearly begun to eye the rest of them and Carrington thought she had had the best idea of the night. With the zorpses de-animated, every link in the five chains surrounding the knoll could concentrate again. Power crackled and spat in arcs and waves toward the sky tear. The fish lords withdrew their appendages as the crack began to close. Someone, most likely Pecca, caused a zipper pull to appear at one end of the crack and slowly, slowly, with all the makers pulling as one, it began to knit the sky back together.

Another rush of wind followed as the crack snapped shut, then the clearing was silent except for hard breathing and Alex's sobbing.

*Audacity?* No, she was there with her poor shaken father, clambering into his arms and rubbing her face against his falling tears. Ras sat with a thump as if his legs wouldn't hold him any longer and Carrington leaned over for a hard hug.

"I'll be right back."

"Carr?"

"Just going up the hill to make certain we're secure."

He had seen Dr. Hayes taken, hadn't he? Still, he approached cautiously, in case the stone circle wasn't empty. When he reached the top, he caught his breath. The circle wasn't entirely empty. Not quite. A white and orange carp flopped in the dirt beside the table — all that remained of Dr. Hayes.

Carefully, Carrington slid his hands under the fish and carried him back down the hill. Yes, what Dr. Hayes had done was unspeakably evil, no matter what his motives. But Carrington had known him since childhood, had fond memories of his library and their conversations. He couldn't bear to watch him gasp out his life in the dust.

No one stopped him, either. When he reached the ornamental pond in the middle of the willows, he crouched down and let the carp slide into the dark water. "Live better, Dr. Hayes. A heron might well eat you, but at least now you have a chance."

He returned to his colleagues as they were regrouping and taking stock. The rens came out of the trees, scraped and bruised here and there, but mostly unharmed. Everyone was dirty and exhausted, the humans among them shivering with cold and Edgar fluffed up into his best puffball.

Lieutenant Dunfee held a hand out to Pecca and waited for her to take it. "Thank you, Ms. Teecosi. We're in your debt. Let's not do this again. Ever."

"Oh, I agree." Pecca nodded, her usually light, cheerful voice hoarse and cracking. "Never would be just fine."

She put an arm around Vance's waist, who didn't blush or pull away this time, and turned him to start back to the cars.

As the rest of them followed suit, Kyle asked, "What the hell are gouramis?"

# Chapter Eight

"Those" — Carrington nodded to the fifty-gallon tank — "are gouramis. Two dwarf, two pearl. The other three I'm not certain about."

"Huh." Kyle bent down for a better look at the delicately patterned fish. "I guess I was expecting something more badass. Like piranhas, maybe. Or undead sharks."

"Terribly sorry to disappoint." Carrington tipped a few flakes of the fish food located beside the tank into the water and watched the fish react with eager zeal. Poor things probably hadn't been fed since before the Night of the Fish Lords.

Cleaning out Dr. Hayes' cottage was taking longer than Carrington would have liked. The job had fallen entirely to the Seventy-Seventh since Captain Valbuena had said his farewells the day after the Piscatory Lord Almost Apocalypse. He had gathered the squad together for a heartfelt speech about a job well done, commendations would be forthcoming for their personnel files, but not public ones for obvious reasons, and so on and so forth. But clean up? No, no, so much work waited for them back in Harrisburg and several of his rens were injured. It was time for them to go.

Carrington didn't shed any tears for their leave taking, but he didn't quite feel the profound sense of relief that he had at the end of previous visits from the captain. Maybe this vampire was growing on him.

While the rooms Carrington remembered fondly from previous visits to Dr. Hayes' cottage were all easily accessible and virtually unchanged for as long as he could recall, every room was also a warren of hidden nooks and alcoves. The second story was worse, with entire rooms warded against discovery. The study, where the gouramis resided, had been one of those.

"Very pretty," Kash murmured, though he remained focused on the stack of books he'd been sorting into piles he'd named *scholarly*, *evil* and *possibly evil in the wrong hands, but informative*. "Does Animal Control take fish?"

"We could ask Jason."

*Possibly evil but interesting* covered a good portion of the hidden material, which they'd dragged out, piece by piece. A team effort, if ever there was one.

Little claws clicked on the hardwood in the hallway and Audacity trotted in, followed closely by her father, who wasn't ready to let her out of his sight. Alex wasn't speaking to LJ yet either. Yes, she'd been instrumental in saving the world, good job, but LJ had smuggled her out of the squad room and put her in danger. Saving the world didn't balance evenly with endangering one's cub in a wolf dad's eyes and arguing that it had been Audacity's idea hadn't helped. LJ had been the adult in that situation, more or less, and Alex would not be moved on that point.

Audacity danced in front of a set of beveled wood panels on the east wall, back and forth, until she stopped in front of one to stand on her hind legs and paw at it.

*Mew! Miiiiiw!*

"That one, sweetie?" Alex tapped a knuckle against what sounded like solid wood.

*Mreh.*

"You're sure this time?"

*Miiii-iiiirrr!*

"I *never* said that. Just making sure you're not rushing." Alex scooped her up, nuzzling at her fur as his voice grew more constricted. "You're smart and wonderful and—" He broke off to call out into the hallway, "Pecca!"

Kyle patted his arm. "She's all right, big guy. Everything turned out okay."

"I know." Alex swiped at his eyes. "I just keep seeing it."

It probably wouldn't have been kind or prudent to tell Alex he most likely would have flashes and dreams of the moment when Audacity landed on a necromancer's head for a long time to come, so Carrington kept his mouth shut.

"Oooh, you found another one!" Pecca cooed as she entered. "Such a good little wolf. Show me what you did."

Audacity squirmed until Alex reluctantly let her down. With a good deal of mewing and running back and forth and sniffing, she related the steps she'd taken. At least that was how it appeared, since Pecca nodded and mm-hmmed here and there.

When Audacity ran out of narrative, Pecca declared, "Perfect! Should we open it?"

*Mew.*

After some tapping and prodding, Pecca pointed a finger at the panel. It melted away to reveal yet another hidden cache in the walls, this one metal-lined and more secure than some of the dusty, cobweb-filled nooks they'd uncovered. Secure, but awkward. Pecca spread her skirts out and knelt so she could twist her shoulders into the alcove and lift the books out one by one.

"Carr, I think you want to see these," Kash said as he relayed the books onto the desk.

"More of the same, I would think," Carrington said with an ill-conceived sigh. *The Munich Necromantic Handbook. Heptameron. Picatrix.* Something clicked in his memory banks. "Ah. I see. I know a certain librarian who will be pleased to see these returned."

"Hope the late fees aren't too bad," Vance said as he strode down the hall carrying a box full of jars — jars full of unspeakable things.

"I didn't — Hilarious, Virago. Just hilarious."

Terrible joke, but Carrington wasn't going to discourage a burgeoning sense of humor that didn't rely on crude insults. Vance had spent a few days in recovery after that night. It hadn't been fair to drag him into it when he'd already been having PTSD episodes, but he was steadying. More and more time spent with Pecca had definitely eased the severity of symptoms.

*Speaking of things a librarian had mentioned, what seems centuries ago now.* "Pecca, what year were you born?"

Pecca still had her head in the hidden alcove, but her answer reached him quite clearly. "Nineteen thirty-two."

"My apologies, Ms. Pecca. I meant you. Not your mother."

She sat back on her heels and gave him an odd look. "That's when I was born. No idea when Mama was born."

Oddly, Carrington wasn't as surprised as he should have been. Kash blinked at her and shrugged, but from the far corner, Kyle muttered, "That's kinda taking cougar to a whole new level."

One last walk through and Pecca declared the house de-necromancered. Not even close to a word, but no one argued. Carrington locked up the house with a pang of regret. Such a lovely place, to be used for such terrible things. Once they had released it from the investigation, the lawyers would move in. Dr. Hayes had no family anyone knew of, nor had anyone been able to locate a will yet.

Carrington leaned against his squad car, parked under the shade of an ancient oak, and called Jason about the fish.

"I wish I could help, Carr. But Animal Control doesn't have the space for a tank that big. And I don't think I have to tell you how Alex would react to it in my house."

"True. Is he doing all right?"

"Mostly. He did try to leave Audacity at home the first couple of days after. She wasn't having it, though. They had some pretty heated arguments." Jason laughed. "And I can't believe I just said that. Look, let me know when you want to move the tank and I'll come help you do it safely. Put it on Craigslist or Nextdoor. Someone will want them."

*For sale by local vampire. One fifty-gallon fish tank with plantings and seven gouramis (various.) Possibly lightly used in necromantic experiments.*

"Perfect. Thank you."

Amanda closed the trunk and came around to the driver's side door. "Library?"

"Yes, please. Maybe I'll regain my hero status in his eyes."

"Don't think he ever stopped thinking of you as a hero. He still being...weird?"

Carrington slumped into the passenger seat. "I haven't been able to figure it out, but I don't want to push him too hard. We talk on the phone. We text. But whenever I ask if he's coming by, he has something else to do."

"You been by his place?"

"Yes, I've driven past when I've known he's home with every intention of stopping and knocking on his door." Carrington let out a half-hearted snort. "I lose my nerve every time. It doesn't seem polite to show up on his doorstep when he wants some distance, not to mention it feels a smidge stalkerish."

"Damn it, Carr. You can't screw this up. Ras is the best thing that ever happened to you."

"Yes. Thank you for reminding me." It was time for a fancy bit of subject changing. "Has Eva approached you?"

Amanda laughed. "Yeah, thought the kid would have a heart attack. But she did."

"She did what? Told you she liked your shoes?"

"No, she asked me out, smartass. Nothing fancy. Just beer and pizza."

"Good. I'm glad. I do like her." Carrington hoped things would stay on an even keel in the squad room, but that horse had run off into the night long ago. "You don't really think of her as a kid, do you?"

"All rookies are kids, Carr. Don't worry. I know she's not *that* much younger than me."

By the time they arrived at the library, the sun was setting, so Carrington was able to take the box of books and carry them instead of fussing with the handcart. The familiar route up the stairs to Rare Books yanked at Carrington's heart every step of the way. He'd been fighting desperately over the past week not to break down when he talked to Ras on the phone, not to let it affect his work and not to dissolve into an abject puddle of despair when someone mentioned his name.

He'd hung on by his fingernails sometimes, but he had been managing. When one of the workers let them through the locked doors and Ras came around the corner, though, Carrington's higher brain functions shut down.

"Hey," Amanda said after an awkward silence. "We found the books?"

Erasmus stared at her as if he'd been startled into noticing her. "Oh. Hi. Books?"

"The ones you reported stolen," Amanda prompted with a roll of her hand.

"Yes, right! Those books." The smile Erasmus offered was strained and uncomfortable. "Great. That's great. Bring them on back. Is it all of them? No. Never mind. That's not appropriate. We'll verify that it's all of them. Of course we will." He had his back to them, so he might have thought he was out of earshot as he muttered, "Babbling. You're babbling. Why did he have to come *here*?"

The ear tugging began and Carrington nearly dropped the box and ran. His presence alone made Ras this anxious and distressed. They followed him into a back room and Carrington set the box down on the table there.

"Okay, so" — Amanda pointed back out to the public spaces of the department — "I'm gonna go visit with the stuffed raven. Come get me when you're done."

*Damn it.* "I hope they're all here," Carrington began, searching for neutral, non-clingy words. "If not, we can go back and look again. We found more than I'd imagined. Ras, I — "

Erasmus held up a hand. "Not here. Carr, please. I've been a coward and avoiding this, I know. I'm sorry. I'll come over after work?"

"It's just — "

"Look, if I start crying at work again, they're going to want to set up counseling and maybe that's not a bad idea, but not right this second, okay?"

Carrington swallowed against the jagged glass in his throat. "All right. I'll…make sure I'm home on time."

Lead. His entire body was turning to lead and he wasn't going to make it out of the room. One impossible step after another, he managed and found Amanda, as promised, by the raven. "Manda, I need…"

"Come on. Let's get you out of here." She took him by the arm and steered him, making sure he didn't smash into doorframes and columns. "What the hell did he say to you?"

"He'll be over tonight to talk."

"Okay, so why's that a bad thing?"

"I believe…" He nearly missed a step as they exited the library, glad of Amanda's vice grip on his arm. "I'm certain this will be the *I can't do this anymore, Carrington* talk."

"'Cause you're always such an optimist." She gave him a little shake. "If it is, it is. But getting yourself all worked up before? Not gonna help."

"I don't know what...I just don't know."

Amanda threw an arm around him and gave him a hard squeeze. "Look, if it's bad, you call me, right? I don't care what time it is."

"All right." He swiped at his eyes before opening the car door. "Manda, I'm sor—"

"I know, okay? How long have I known you?"

Carrington did manage to get through the last hour of shift, drive home and get changed without falling apart. Then he sat in the dark waiting for the by-now familiar sound of the key in the lock. After a few moments brooding, that struck him as creepy, so he turned the living room lights on for a better brooding ambiance.

At six-thirty, when he was considering how vampirism might affect brooding expertise, footsteps sounded on the stairs followed by keys jingling as Ras searched for the right one on his ring.

"Hey." Ras managed a wan smile when he came through the door.

"Hi." Carrington's voice wavered on the first word. *This isn't going to go well.*

Ras closed the door and hurried across the room to wrap Carrington in a bone-creaking hug. Carrington held his breath. If he took a breath, the waterworks would start. He couldn't. Just couldn't.

"I'm so sorry. Gods. I didn't mean to torture you. But I've been torturing me." Ras rubbed Carrington's back frantically as if he could somehow keep them both in one piece that way. "I needed time. Time to think on my own. I'm so crazy about you, it's hard to think straight around you sometimes."

"I'll…" Carrington laid his head on the bony shoulder he'd missed so much. "I'll do my best not to make anything hard for you."

"Okay, look. It started a while ago, but it just crept up on me. Worrying about you at work. Worrying—anyway, that's not where I was going. I know your work is dangerous. Not like I haven't been caught up in it before. But this last thing, The Night of the Interdimensional Fish Lords, that wasn't just random monsters. That was end of the world stuff. The world was going to *end*, along with you and all the people I love."

"Not my favorite night either, I'll be honest."

Ras pushed him back to see his face. "Carr, I was quietly freaking out. Alex was in tears. Vance had a bad episode and ended up curled in a ball on the ground. But you? You looked around to make sure everyone was in one piece and *walked up that damn hill*. Like the sky hadn't just cracked up there. Like a sorcerer wasn't trying to let alien monsters in. You strolled up there and picked up the sorcerer who'd been turned into a damn fish like it was just another day."

Carrington stared, completely flummoxed. "It didn't *feel* like that."

Ras took both his hands in a tight grip. "Okay. Trying again. I'm not faulting you for being brave and badass because you are. And that's your job. But that was my mistake. It's not my job. I'm a librarian and I let myself get tangled up in your world so far that I scared the hell out of myself. No, that's not even right. I insisted on getting tangled in your world, even when you begged me not to."

"You helped us enormously. We couldn't have done all we did without you."

"I'm glad I could. Part of me is." Ras ducked his head, swallowing hard. "But after that night, it kept running around in my head so hard I couldn't sleep. I kept thinking *I can't do this*. I can't be so in love with someone who goes out into that kind of danger every day, the kind I can't wave off anymore when I've seen it firsthand."

"I understand." Carrington rubbed his thumb over the back of one of those beloved hands, corpse white against the healthy, human brown of Erasmus' skin. Of course this couldn't work. Doomed from the start. "I do love you so. And I need you to do what makes you happy. Whole."

The laugh that got away from Ras was harsh and desperate. "After all that, you think I'm here to tell you I'm walking away? Gods. Carr. I talked a long time to my moms this afternoon. They told me what I knew. That I was being a dumbass. That when you love a cop, that's what you do — kiss them goodbye in the morning and thank all the powers when they come home at night. So I had to ask myself if I could keep doing that. It's that or I'd have to give you up. But I can't live in your world that much again. I can't. I'm a librarian, not a hero who walks up evil hills with dead actors dying a second time all around him. I'm talking way too much…"

"That last thing," Carrington said into the sudden silence. "Was difficult for all of us. There's quite a bit of counseling going on. I…haven't gone. Oddly, I haven't felt up to it, and isn't that ridiculous? But I'm confused here. Are you breaking up with me or not?"

"I'm trying not to. If you're not completely repelled and frustrated by now."

"On a scale of repulsion, you rate about a minus twenty for me." Carrington pressed both Erasmus' hands to his lips. "I've missed you so. And I'm more than happy for you *not* to be involved in my work again, thank you very much. Research help, I'll take at any point. The actual having you in harm's way part, my heart can do without."

"Well, good. I have to say it again—I'm sorry it took me a while to get my head around things. But that's why I called you every night. I didn't want you to think I'd just walked away."

"It was...a lot to process. Not something I can fault you for. I do have to confess, I like it better when you're here in person, though." Carrington's insides were still shaky, his head wobbly as if it weren't attached on quite right, so in that moment of tilting axes, he took a daring leap. "It always makes me feel better to know you'll be here. Do you think, perhaps, not that I'm rushing you, that it's time to move in with me?"

Erasmus pulled him close and held on tight, his tears falling on Carrington's neck. "I think I'd like that, Officer Loveless. But we're using my small appliances. Your toaster sucks and your coffeemaker's tragic."

"Duly noted."

"And we have to do something about your *I just use this place to sleep* décor."

"I bow to your better judgment."

Ras tapped him on the chest with two fingers. "And you're never skipping a meal again."

"But—"

"Vampires who fight monsters need their nutrition."

"I'll do my best. Though my fondest hope is that we've seen the last of the truly strange monsters now." Carrington stroked a thumb along Erasmus' jaw. "As for the combining of domestic lives, I'm flexible in all things."

"You are pretty flexible." Ras nudged until Carrington reclined on the sofa, then snuggled in with his head on Carrington's chest. "I do love you, you know. In case I forgot that part in everything else."

"It's nice to hear the words, though I did know. We're going to end up at two Thanksgiving dinners this year, aren't we?" Carrington kissed the top of Erasmus' head, his heart finally calming as the books and spice scent of his librarian surrounded him.

"Hmm, probably." Ras snuggled closer and pulled the blanket off the back of the sofa to cover them. "We'll figure it out. Don't worry about it now."

Carrington managed the first smile in days and took what felt like the first deep breath as well. Surrender. There were a thousand ways in which he could and he was determined to delight in each and every one.

# Quinn's Gambit

## *Excerpt*

## Chapter One

*Surely just a kiss, an embrace… These things can only be beneficial.* Valerian let his hands slide down the lovely human boy's back. He leaned in to press his lips against those full, lush ones offered up to him so willingly…

Perhaps it was the human scent or the way the boy ground against him a bit too eagerly. None of it was right or familiar, all of the foreign human-ness grating on his nerves. He pulled away and turned to face the window, arms crossed over his chest.

"I'm sorry. This isn't working."

"You telling me this was a waste of my time? You drag me all the way up here for nothing? Time's money, big boy."

Val ground his back teeth together, fighting his temper. "I neither break nor bend my promises. Your money is there, on the bureau. You may take it and leave me."

"Hey." The sharp voice calmed to something more soothing. A gentle hand caressed his arm. "I didn't mean it like that. Just gotta be careful, you know? We don't have to do anything. I have clients that just wanna talk or cuddle. I have one who just wants someone to hold him while he cries."

*Is that what I'll soon be reduced to? Paying someone to comfort me?* "I spoke harshly. I apologize. But I have... It was a mistake. Please. I occupied your time. The money is yours. I simply need to be alone now."

"Okay. I get it. But you change your mind, you call me, yeah?" The boy shoved the roll of cash into the pocket of his threadbare jeans. "Give me a chance to see if those yummy pointed elf ears are as sensitive as they say."

With a grin and a wink, he swaggered out of the room. A moment later, the door to the apartment clicked shut. Val leaned his forehead against the cool glass, gazing down at the late evening traffic ten floors below. He could open the window. Lean out. Tumble to the waiting pavement.

Val heaved a weary sigh. A human would die, but with his bone structure, he was likely to survive — in a good deal of pain, but still alive. Living alone had begun to wear on him, nothing more. Perhaps he should have a roommate. It wasn't the same as having a *senrist* of young males waiting for him, but at least it would be someone with whom to converse. Gods, but he missed them. He had tried to describe the *senrist* to his human work partner once. The closest parallel he could pull up had been a harem, but it didn't begin to convey the love and devotion he had once been so privileged to have.

There were days he felt better, days when he thought, perhaps, he could adjust. Then something like this would happen to remind him that this was not his world. He would never belong here. The city bustled below him, sunlit streets and people hurrying about their days. Life—all around him life—while every day he died a bit more inside.

* * * *

Quinn sat on the sunny park bench watching ducks paddle around in the pond a few feet away. He had been sitting enjoying the warm weather and waiting for just over an hour when a young mother walked by with a toddler clutching her hand. An older boy tagged along beside them. Both kids had ice cream cones, the little girl with most of hers on her hands and face and down the front of her shirt, but she was still adorable in springy, golden pigtails.

Quinn watched as the family made their way down the path toward the footbridge that crossed the duck pond. They seemed completely unaware of the dark shape moving under the water, tracking their progress. Just before they reached the bridge, the dark shape resolved, lurching up out of the water. A tangle of weed, muck and pond scum streamed down a huge face twisted into a monstrous grimace, and the creature gave a low, menacing growl.

"Shit!" Quinn muttered and shot off the bench. This was not supposed to happen.

The mother and children screamed, their ice cream cones flying as they raced away from the bridge in the other direction. Quinn knew they were headed directly toward a cul-de-sac that ended in high shrubs, a fence and nowhere to run.

The monster lumbered out of the pond, growling, gnashing its pointed teeth, arms outstretched as it went after the terrified family. Quinn was faster, though, and raced down the path, darting between the monster and its intended prey. The woman had just figured out she had run right into a dead end and was trapped. She clutched the crying kids and they huddled together, terrified.

"Don't worry. I'll protect you!" Quinn yelled, boldly turning toward the reeking beast. He raised his staff, muttering an indecipherable incantation. The end of the staff began to glow brightly and he pointed it at the pond monster. "Begone! Leave these people alone, foul beast!"

The creature hesitated, then took a few more menacing steps.

"I said, begone!" Quinn shouted, brandishing the staff. "I warn you…if I release the fireball from my staff, you will not survive it, fell creature!" *Begone… Fell creature… God, I feel so cheesy saying stuff like that.*

The swamp monster came to a shambling halt. Groaning, it lifted its gray-green, seaweed-draped arm to shield itself from the light that glowed bright from the end of the staff. With a cry that sounded as if it were afraid and in pain, it started to back away. Quinn followed, keeping the staff thrust forward, driving the creature back. At last it fled, shuffling back to the pond and sinking into the murky water.

Quinn breathed a sigh of relief and let the energy drain out of the spell. The glow at the end of the staff winked out. He turned back to the shaken family.

"It's okay. It's gone now. It won't bother you again," he said in his most confident and soothing voice.

"Oh, God, thank you! Thank you so much! I don't know what we would have done if you hadn't been here." Tears of relief shimmered in the woman's eyes now that it looked like she and her children were safe.

"You don't look like a wizard," the boy said, looking up at Quinn with huge round eyes. "You look like my brother, Robbie. He's in high school and thinks he's too good to play games anymore."

Quinn managed a smile. "I'm a little older than that. Every wizard was young once, though. Good thing I was here today or that troll would have had you guys for lunch."

"You'd think those people from AURA would make sure beasts like that were locked up! I don't know how I can repay you," the mother gushed, already reaching into her pocketbook.

Quinn held his hand up, "No, no, I couldn't. It's no more than anyone would have done. It's quite all right," he said humbly.

"I insist, please. At least let me buy you lunch." She pressed the bills into his hand.

Quinn hesitated and finally closed his hand around the money. Bowing his head graciously, he made the cash disappear, this time with sleight of hand rather than real magic.

"Let me escort you past the pond so I know you've made it safely out of the park. Then I'll go back and see if I can hold the monster until AURA gets here," Quinn said.

He led the grateful family away, over the bridge and back toward the street, making sure they were in a more populous area before he took his leave. On his way back to the pond, he stopped at a hot dog cart and bought four footlongs with some of the money the woman had given him.

The pond's surface was smooth as glass when he returned, no sign of the monster or people anywhere. He waited, listening. He walked up the path about twenty yards, checking for any pedestrians, then walked back. "All right, coast is clear," he said to empty air.

The 'monster', who wasn't a troll at all but a boggle, rose up out of the depths, face split in a gruesome smile.

Quinn put a hand on his hip and looked at him sternly. "I thought we agreed you'd wait until I gave you the signal?"

"Aw, c'mon, Quinten. That was the most fun I've had in ages!" the boggle said.

"I said no marks with kids, Groof! They'll probably have nightmares for months!"

"Oh, listen to you, Mr. Moral High Ground." Groof snorted, which sent a spray of pond water from his nostrils. "What about that octogenarian you signaled on last week? He could have had a heart attack. Besides, the old ones don't run nearly as fast." He laughed, a wet sound, as if mud was stuck in his throat.

Quinn sighed. "Next time, *wait for the signal,* Groof. Here..." He tossed the hot dogs one at a time, still wrapped in paper, into Groof's open maw, saving the last for himself. He tried not to grimace as the boggle chewed open-mouthed and his black tongue licked not just his lips but also his chin, cheeks and nostrils after swallowing each one. Groof was cool as far as boggles went and he was a pretty good partner, but his eating habits made Quinn a little queasy.

"Mmm... Extra mustard and onions, just like I wanted. You are a good friend, Quinten," Groof rumbled with a happy chortle.

"Yeah, yeah... All right. See you tomorrow." Quinn sent him an airy wave over his shoulder as he hefted his backpack and started in on his own hot dog on his way out of the park.

# About the Author

The unlikely black sheep of an ivory tower intellectual family, Angel Martinez has managed to make her way through life reasonably unscathed. Despite a wildly misspent youth, she snagged a degree in English Lit, married once and did it right the first time, (same husband for almost twenty-four years) gave birth to one amazing son, (now in college) and realized at some point that she could get paid for writing.

Published since 2006, Angel's cynical heart cloaks a desperate romantic. You'll find drama and humor given equal weight in her writing and don't expect sad endings. Life is sad enough.

She currently lives in Delaware in a drinking town with a college problem and writes Science Fiction and Fantasy centered around gay heroes.

Angel Martinez loves to hear from readers. You can find her contact information, website details and author profile page at http://www.pride-publishing.com.

www.ingramcontent.com/pod-product-compliance
Lightning Source LLC
Chambersburg PA
CBHW020421180626
46812CB00003B/1088